"You're just being deliberately dense!"

"Wherever your brains are, they certainly don't reach your feet!" Sean snapped.

Sarah wrenched herself away. "I told you I couldn't dance," she said angrily. "Perhaps you'll believe me now. F-find yourself another partner." She headed for the door.

Sean was there before her, grasping her arm. "I've already got one. The trouble with you is you like your own way. Let yourself go," he commanded.

Sarah was past arguing, past a lot of things, particularly attempting to dance. She stood stock-still.

The next moment she was in his arms and he was kissing her with a frightening ferocity.

Then just as abruptly, he released her with an expression of disgust. "Now see what you've done," he shouted. "Get the hell out of here before I lose all sense of proportion!"

These books may be available at your local bookseller.

Don't miss any of our special offers. Write to us at the following address for information on our newest releases.

Harlequin Reader Service
P.O. Box 52040, Phoenix, AZ 85072-2040
Canadian address: P.O. Box 2800, Postal Station A,
5170 Yonge St., Willowdale, Ont. M2N 6J3

Cartier's Strike

Jane Corrie

Harlequin Books

TORONTO • NEW YORK • LONDON
AMSTERDAM • PARIS • SYDNEY • HAMBURG
STOCKHOLM • ATHENS • TOKYO • MILAN

Original hardcover edition published in 1985
by Mills & Boon Limited

ISBN 0-373-02743-5

Harlequin Romance first edition February 1986

CHAPTER ONE

'WHY didn't you tell me who you were?' Sean Cartier demanded harshly to Sarah Helm, who stood regarding him, her sapphire blue eyes holding a hint of anxiousness in them.

'I didn't know about your connection with Don,' she replied in a low voice. 'He didn't tell me much about his relations. In any case, it was a long time ago,' she added defensively.

Sean's dark brooding glance swept over her diminutive five foot two, and rested briefly on her honey-gold hair, cut close to her head, framing her heart-shaped face. 'Don't give me that,' he growled. 'You're not trying to tell me that a bright reporter like you didn't know of the connection. Oh, no, you knew all right, you just miscalculated on the strength of your charms. I suppose the rest of your pals out there have been having a good laugh at my expense.'

'That's not true,' Sarah replied quietly. 'No one else knows, I can assure you. As I said, it's a long time ago, and it's something I wanted to forget. I'm not likely to have mentioned it to anyone,' her smooth forehead creased in a frown. 'I don't know how——'

'How I found out?' sneered Sean. 'That seems to be another of your miscalculations. Let's say a little bird told me. I can understand your reasons for not wanting to broadcast the past. You wouldn't be half so damn popular with that lot out there if they knew what you'd done to Don, that's for sure!'

Sarah's fine eyes blazed back at him. Now she was angry. What right had he to condemn her? What did he know of the matter? 'You've no right to set yourself up as judge and jury,' she said coldly. 'I don't know what you've heard, but there's another side to it.' She drew in a long breath. 'I'm perfectly willing to tell you my side of the story, if you'll listen,' she told him, her anger now abated. She'd suffered a lot in the past, blaming herself for the tragedy, until some good friends had talked some sense into her.

'I'll bet you are!' Sean bit back caustically at her. 'Only I prefer to use my own judgment. I knew my cousin pretty well, you see. Okay, so he liked a good time, and was a little too fond of the bottle, but that doesn't excuse your treatment of him. Any woman worth her salt would have pulled him round, and from what I heard he was crazy enough about you to have mended his ways, but you sent him over that cliff as sure as if you'd pushed him.' He nodded at Sarah's wince at this bald pronouncement. 'No, it's not a pretty story, is it? It's no wonder you prefer to forget it, but I've got a long memory, Miss Helm, and I'm not likely to forget or forgive.'

His eyes narrowed as he surveyed her. 'You've been on this site for three days,' he said harshly. 'You had ample opportunity to explain things then, but you kept quiet, didn't you? My invitations to dinner must have amused you immensely, but I'm afraid your luck didn't hold.

Now you dance to my tune, got that?' he added savagely.

Sarah's white face said that she had got it, and she knew that it was hopeless to try to convince him that she truly had not known that he was Don's cousin. If she had known, she thought bleakly, wild horses wouldn't have dragged her to this barren area of the Northern Territory, possible huge oil strike or no. They could have struck diamonds as large as ostrich eggs for that matter, she still wouldn't have come. She drew herself up to her full height, and met his scathing eyes with complete frankness in hers. 'I'll get my editor to replace me,' she said quietly.

'You'll do no such thing!' Sean thundered at her. 'No one else is coming on this site, and that's flat!'

For a moment Sarah thought that he was willing to let her go on with her assignment, and a small ray of hope gleamed in her eyes, but his next words dashed her expectations.

'You're staying until the project is over, but I'm not having you at the press conferences. You can pick up what gleanings your pals out there will let drop your way, and I don't think it's going to be much. Not with my experience of the newspaper hounds. It's their reputations and scoops that come first, isn't it?' he sneered. 'And you'll not know whether what they do tell you is true, will you?' he added meaningly.

Sarah's lovely eyes showed her indignation. 'That's unfair!' she snapped angrily. 'So you don't want me around, but to take it out on my paper is despicable. Let me at least get in touch with my editor,' the last words were spoken in a soft almost pleading voice, Sarah was not one to beg, but this was her job, and a good one, and she had been chosen to cover this assignment because of her flair for following up the small print and coming up with the goods, that had earned her the nickname of 'Sarah Scoop' by her office compatriots in tolerant amusement.

'By all means,' Sean said loftily, and jerked an arm towards the phone on his desk. 'It might be as well to let him know that his ace reporter has fallen down on the job.'

Sarah took a deep breath, and moved quickly over to the desk. Somehow, Eddie Lyall had to get someone else out there, and fast, or they'd lose out on what could be the story of the year. Sean Cartier had been right in presuming that precious little would be passed on to her. There was a limit to friendship where careers were involved. She heard Eddie's growled, 'News Editor,' and plunged in with, 'Eddie, Sarah here. Look, I'm being taken off the story. I can't explain over the phone, and Mr Cartier doesn't seem willing to replace me—could you——?'

That was as far as she was allowed to get before the receiver was yanked out of her hand. 'Cartier here,' Sean said in a harsh voice. 'Just confirming Miss Helm's call. Don't try and replace your journalist. They won't get past the main gates. As you well know, the ones that are here got on to the site without authority, but I'm willing to stretch a point and let them stay, but that's as far as I'm going.'

Sarah could almost hear Eddie bursting a blood

vessel on the other end of the line, but could do nothing about it. As much as he thought of Sarah's work, he was not likely to forgive her for letting him down on an assignment as big as this one. In her mind's eye she saw herself tramping the circuits of their rivals' offices, looking for work.

Sean Cartier carefully replaced the telephone in the middle of the rapid exchange being fired from her boss's end, and gave Sarah a wolf-like grin of pure satisfaction. 'Goes on a bit, doesn't he?' he commented. 'He ought to be more choosy in picking his staff.'

Sarah wanted to throw the desk memorandum at him, but didn't think it would be worth the effort, and walked to the door of the office.

'Just one small matter, Miss Helm,' he said, almost purring in his pleasure at a thought he had just had. 'We're not likely to get any results through for several days yet, and while I don't mind providing food and lodgings for the rest of the press, they have their job to do, don't they? I don't feel at all charitable where you're concerned. I've heard they're hard up for help in the kitchen—all these extra men, you know,' he added conversationally. 'If it's not beneath your dignity, perhaps you could help out? At least you'll be paying for your keep, won't you?'

Sarah's eyes acknowledged that last order, for it was an order, with more aplomb than she felt, but she had her pride and it saw her through. She gave a small nod, and said, 'Very well, Mr Cartier. I'll try to give satisfaction,' in a voice that suggested that she had just landed a plum job and wanted to show her appreciation.

It worked, and she had the satisfaction of seeing Sean Cartier's eyes blaze back at her. 'You'd damn well better,' he snarled at her. 'I'll have no loafers on this site!'

On this cheerful if slightly menacing conclusion of the interview, Sarah left his office and made her way back to the room she was sharing with Martha Smart, who worked for her father's press agency, aptly named 'Get Smart', and who was the last person Sarah would have wanted to pass on the news of her demotion from journalist to scullery maid, for Martha was jealous of Sarah for two good reasons—one, that Sarah had looks, and two, that she was intelligent, and better at her job than Martha could ever be, who had neither looks nor compensating genius, and held her position purely through her doting father's indulgence.

'What did he want to see you about?' asked Martha, pouncing on Sarah as soon as she entered the room that smelt like a beauty parlour and looked it, with Martha's beauty aids spilled over the makeshift dressing table.

Sarah threw her shoulder bag that contained her notebook ready at all times to take a statement down on to her bed and made a wry face, which was immediately misinterpreted by Martha.

'Come on! We all know you're teacher's pet,' she said spitefully. 'You might as well tell me. You can't release anything yet, not until he gives the go-ahead, and we shall know at the lunchtime confab he's holding anyway. Have they found the stuff or not?' she demanded.

Sarah took a deep breath. 'I don't know——'
she began hesitantly.

'Don't give me that!' Martha bit out. 'I don't
believe you. No wonder you're the star of the
Daily! All you've got to do is blink those blue
eyes of yours in a certain direction, and you get
the scoop, don't you?' she added waspishly.

'Shut up, Martha!' Sarah replied wearily,
wiping the sceptical expression off Martha's face.
Sarah was not one to snap back like that. All in
all, she was usually maddeningly calm when
Martha tried to get a rise out of her. 'If you want
the truth, there'll be no scoops coming my way
on this assignment. In fact, I've been taken off
the press list.'

Martha stared at her, her too brightly painted
mouth agape and her pale blue eyes blinking in
disbelief, then she nodded as an explanation
occurred to her, reminding Sarah of a Chinese
Mandarin doll that she had been fond of when a
child. 'Ahah! Things got too hot for you, did
they?' Martha exclaimed, unable to keep the note
of pure satisfaction out of her voice. 'I could have
told you not to play around with the big boss.
He's not in the little boys' league, you know. I've
got a friend who tangled with him some years
ago, got to dreaming about weddings and all that
nonsense. Did she get a shock!' Martha savoured
that last bit with a smug grimness. 'So, as I said,
that type doesn't give anything away, not without
collecting—and I mean collecting.'

'Oh, do shut up, Martha!' Sarah repeated
stonily. 'It's not like that at all,' and she glared at
Martha, who was grinning slyly. 'There are other

things in life, you know, apart from sex, although you're going to find it hard to believe.' She took a deep breath. 'It's about something that happened a long time ago, and concerns someone he once knew. Someone he felt I let down. He's only just found out about the connection, and I didn't know of it either, or else I wouldn't have come— but got someone else to cover the story for us. Now he won't even consider a replacement—says that I'll have to rely on the others for information.'

One part of Martha was digesting the news, the other part, the journalistic training part, was quick to see an opportunity. 'You give me all the gen you've got so far,' she said, 'and I'll pass on whatever I hear at the confab,' she suggested eagerly.

Write her copy for her, in other words, Sarah thought dispassionately. 'I know no more than you do,' she said quietly, holding on to her temper.

Martha pouted in disbelief. 'So you keep telling me,' she said, 'but I don't believe you. You're too much of a newshound to let any opportunity pass. Okay, don't tell me. You'll have to rely on the men for your story, won't you? I should have a go at Charles Ashley, he's got a soft spot for you, hasn't he?' she suggested spitefully.

Sarah shrugged her slim shoulders. Charles would be the last one she would ask for help, he definitely came into the category of not giving anything away without expecting suitable reward, and Sarah had a good idea of what he would consider suitable. He was always throwing invitations her way, but Sarah knew a little too much about him to accept his dubious offer of a quiet dinner at his flat.

'So what will you do? Go back?' asked Martha, summoning up a happy picture of herself as the only female on the project, and all the gorgeous problems that could present themselves stuck out as they were in the lonely outback region they had landed in.

Unwittingly Sarah broke her pretty balloon. 'I only wish I could! No, I'm staying. I've no choice in the matter—I've been assigned kitchen duties,' she made a face. 'He doesn't see why I shouldn't earn my keep,' she added wryly.

Martha's mouth fell open. 'Boy, he has got it in for you, hasn't he?' she commented, unable to keep the gleeful note out of her voice. 'What on earth did you do? Murder someone?' she asked in high amusement.

Sarah's lovely eyes took on a bleak look. It was too near the truth to be shrugged off lightly. She had already said too much to Martha, but she knew only too well that with a little digging Martha could find out, so it was better to have it over and done with. It was bad enough being accused of sending someone to their death without having the threat of exposure hanging over her, because Martha wouldn't be the only one to start wondering. Newsmen were naturally curious and could smell a story a mile away. 'From where Sean Cartier's sitting, that's just about his view of what happened,' Sarah said wearily. 'I was engaged to a cousin of his—this was five years ago, then I found out that he was playing around with someone else, so I broke it off, and he got drunk and drove his car off a cliff.' She met Martha's avid expression, obviously wanting to hear all the gory details, but Sarah had no intention of supplying any more than the basic facts.

'No wonder Cartier's ardour was cooled,' Martha commented baldly, seeing nothing offensive in this remark, since it was plain to see what she had thought Sarah and Sean Cartier had been up to during those dinners they had shared in Sean's private quarters, for that was the way Martha looked at life.

Sarah knew this, but did not hold it against her, not even when she was feeling so low. It was a natural conclusion, and she presumed that Martha hadn't been the only one to reach it. Charles Ashley, for another, had probably been thinking on those same lines, but it hadn't been like that at all, not that anyone would believe her.

A voice then came over the intercom—a voice that Sarah knew only too well, 'Would all members of the press attend a conference in the main dining area in precisely ten minutes' time. Miss Helm to report to Mrs Pullman in the canteen.'

Sarah bent down and picked up her shoulder bag off the bed, and met Martha's amused eyes as she straightened up. 'He doesn't do things by half, does he?' she commented, trying not to let a note of bitterness creep into her voice. In one short announcement he had told the rest of the press that she was no longer regarded as a bona

fide representative of her paper, and to add insult
to injury, had given her her marching orders to
the canteen.

'You're not going to work in the canteen, are
you?' asked Martha in amusement. 'Not the star
reporter of the *Daily News!*'

Sarah walked to the door. 'I'd rather do that
than suffer charity from a man who can see only
one side of the story,' she said quietly, and left
Martha to her over-stimulated imagination.

It would not surprise her, Sarah thought, if she
were to find herself allocated to a different
section of the works, where the manual workers
were housed on the site, pushed back out of the
mainstream of events with their own social
quarters. So much secrecy surrounded the site,
because it wasn't only oil Sean Cartier was
seeking. His very presence at a site meant there
was something big brewing, only all that had
been released so far was that oil was there, and
ostensibly that it was on a large enough scale to
warrant commercial enterprise. This was news in
itself, for the country needed the oil, but there
was no getting away from the fact that Sean
Cartier was on the spot, and held a high position
in the Bureau of Mineral Resources, and his
presence acted like a magnet to any self-
respecting journalist, whatever was put out on a
government handout to the press.

Sarah reached the canteen without meeting
anyone she knew, for which she was devoutly
grateful. She could imagine the speculation going
around in the small bar at the end of the large
dining hall area where they usually gathered

before a press conference, and was doubly relieved that the kitchen was cut off from the dining hall and all the food was sent down in lifts, so she would be saved the embarrassment of having the others watching her at work— embarrassment on both sides, really, because on the whole they were a decent lot, Sarah mused, as she went up the steps that led to the busy kitchen and looked around for the said Mrs Pullman.

A flustered-looking young girl with an apron two sizes too big for her gave her a quick annoyed look that plainly asked what she thought she was doing there, and that this was where the workers plied their trade, and she didn't want anyone standing watching her at work, thank you. Just then a plump, rather formidable-looking woman, also in an apron and cap, thrust the girl aside and enquired tartly, 'Are you Miss Helm?'

Sarah acknowledged that that was her name, and decided to ignore the sniff of disapproval from Mrs Pullman, since that was who the enquirer must have been, as she gave her a good looking over, taking in Sarah's tailored silk suit and matching business-styled blouse. 'You'll have to wear something over that,' she commented disapprovingly, and sighed loudly. 'As if I hadn't enough to cope with,' she said, and glared at the young girl standing by and listening avidly to the conversation. 'Lunch in thirty minutes,' she said crisply, 'and we're not getting on with it, are we, Sandy? Away with you! I want the rest of those potatoes peeled in fifteen minutes flat,' she ordered, as the girl scuttled away back to the huge sink at the end of the kitchen where a mound of peeled potatoes ready for the pot filled a huge white bowl. She then directed her attention back to Sarah in a tired way that suggested that she hoped she would somehow have disappeared, and gave another loud sigh on finding that Sarah was still there. 'Well, I suppose you can get on with the washing up of the used pans,' she nodded towards another sink a little bit further along the wall, glaring at Sarah. 'No objection, I hope?' she dared her.

Sarah shook her head. 'No objection, Mrs Pullman,' she replied lightly, and looked around for an overall that was quickly supplied by the manageress, with an air of slight surprise at Sarah's willingness to oblige, and who clearly thought that there must be a catch in it somewhere, and that nobody told her anything.

By the end of lunch, Sarah's hands were a little on the red side, having been constantly immersed in hot sudded water, for she had stayed with the washing up chore until all the luncheon dishes were cleared. Her feet encased in elegant brogues ached from the constant standing, and caused her to give way to a sardonic grin at the thought that she had thought that she was pretty fit, but it only took an unusual job to prove otherwise.

For her devotion to duty she earned Mrs Pullman's grudging praise, then she found herself up to her elbows in vegetables to be got ready for dinner, by which time her back had joined her feet in aching protest at the enforced maltreatment, and when the vegetables were finished, and Mrs Pullman announced that she could take two hours off, but report back to work at six-thirty, all Sarah wanted to do was to lie flat on her bed, hoping for physical recovery before the next onslaught, and as soon as she got back to her quarters that was precisely what she did, and was thankful for the fact that Martha was not around to witness her exhaustion, because that would have been more than she could take at that time.

She had to stay fit, she thought, as she lay with closed eyes soaking up the luxury of relief from her aches and pains. No way was she going to back out on the excuse of physical exhaustion, for she could well imagine Sean Cartier's caustic comments on what he would consider skiving on her part.

The first day was always the worst, wasn't it? she told herself firmly. It was just that she wasn't used to the continual standing, but by tomorrow she would be all right. She felt the glare of the late afternoon sun on her eyelids, but hadn't the energy to get up and pull down the blinds at the window. What luxury a good soak in a bath would be now, she thought longingly, but there were no such refinements on the site. Showers, of course, and Sarah would have to take one before she reported for duty again, but not yet, she told herself; she didn't have to move yet.

Now that she could relax, her mind went over the sudden change of circumstances. Things had happened too fast for her to really take in, and she had been given no previous warning that a spectre from the past would rear its ugly head again to disturb her peace.

There was no way she could have known that

Sean Cartier was Don's cousin, as Don had been reticent about his family, and Sarah, who had been orphaned at an early age and reared by an aunt, had thought that, like her, he had had an unhappy childhood, and had not sought confirmation.

It hadn't mattered in those early days, when Sarah was a very junior reporter on the local newspaper, and had met Don at a wedding she was attending for the paper. She sighed. She had been eighteen then, and very eager to make her mark in her chosen profession. Don had worked for a big advertising agency that had thrown a lot of work her paper's way. It had all been so wonderful at the time, she thought, recalling the day the editor congratulated her on obtaining such a prized contract, for as with most provincial papers they relied heavily on revenue from advertisements to keep their heads above water, and their small paper needed it more than most.

She turned her head restlessly, as if to dismiss the past, but she couldn't. Not now that it had caught up with her again. Had she really loved Don? The thought had haunted her for a long time after his death, and she had come to the sad conclusion that she hadn't. If she had, she would still be mourning his death, and still looking for an excuse to blame herself for what had happened.

Sarah drew a deep breath. Don had been weak, and he couldn't resist a drink, neither could he resist a pretty woman. Not that that alone would have killed what she had thought was her love for him. No, it had been much worse than that, for when Don had proposed to her and been accepted by the deliriously happy Sarah, he had had a mistress tucked away downtown, living in deplorable conditions and supporting a young child—his child.

It was only by a stroke of fate that Sarah had found out about it. She had been covering a funeral and had visited the poorer area of the town to get the details from the relatives, and found herself sitting in a dingy top flat staring at a photograph of Don holding a young boy in his arms and laughing at the camera.

After the first sense of shock had worn off, Sarah gave no sign of recognising the man in the picture. Even if she had, it would not have been noticed by the woman supplying the details for the press, she was too upset at the loss of her only surviving parent to notice any unusual behaviour on the part of the young reporter, but a few innocent-sounding queries from Sarah gave her all the confirmation she needed.

Confirmation that hadn't really been necessary after a child about four years old had rushed into the room and clung to his mother's skirts. His wide brown eyes, so like his father's, had quashed any hope of Sarah's that Don might just have been a friend of the family.

Sarah drew in a quick breath. At that time, she supposed, she must have been in love with Don, for she had tried to excuse him. The woman was pretty, with fair naturally curly hair, and a plump curvaceous figure that would attract men—not that she looked her best when Sarah saw her, for sorrow had left her pinched-looking and touch-ingly pathetic.

It had only taken a few sympathetic words for everything to come tumbling out, and an embarrassed Sarah didn't want to hear her story, not when she wanted to exonerate Don; but she had to listen, and as she did so, her love for Don evaporated into thin air.

It was the old, old story. The man, she was given to understand, was married, and couldn't get a divorce, and couldn't really afford to keep two homes going, and she had to survive on the pittance he sent her or brought her whenever he could get away.

Sarah recalled feeling physically sick as she stumbled down the dingy staircase and out into the blessed sweetness of the morning air. She was not naïve, she knew that men did this sort of thing, but she found it hard to understand how any woman could be so taken in, although she had to concede that Don was a charmer, and too good-looking for his own good. Women adored him. The only thing Sarah could not forgive was his meanness. He was earning a high salary, and could well afford to keep his mistress and their child in better circumstances, but had preferred to adopt a deplorable ploy to cover his meanness.

Totally honest herself, Sarah had no time for such dishonesty, particularly when it affected the welfare of children, and she had it out with Don that very evening. He did not deny the charge. It would not have been any good if he had, but he did try to excuse himself on the grounds of being very young when he had met the girl; he had got caught up in a situation he abhorred but could do nothing about, which might have worked had Sarah not actually seen the woman and the conditions she was living in, or more to the point, known that Don was still in the habit of visiting her.

The meeting had ended with Sarah throwing his ring back at him and telling him in no uncertain terms that she wanted nothing more to do with him.

A day later, Don's car was found on the rocks below a point where they had once used to sit in the evenings discussing their future. He had been killed outright, and although the verdict was accidental death, most of Sarah's acquaintances had been sure that he had committed suicide.

At first, the devastated Sarah had thought the same, but as time went on she accepted the original verdict. Don had been drinking heavily and had taken a bend too fast. There was also the salient fact that he had enjoyed life too much to let a broken engagement alter his outlook, for he had cockily predicted that she would be back within a week, begging his forgiveness, which he might or might not give.

It was as well for Sarah that she did have some good friends around her at this time. Friends who had sounded a warning note on her engagement to Don. 'Once a womaniser, always a womaniser,' one blunt friend had commented, and although deep down Sarah had known this, she had preferred to stick her head in the sand until the thunderbolt had struck and made her face up to reality.

Sarah's thoughts roamed on, and turned to other matters, such as what her editor was cooking up at his end, in fact, anything to take her mind off the past. That was over and done with, or had been, until she had come up against Sean Cartier. She forced this thought away. She simply couldn't see Eddie Lyall accepting Cartier's dictates, he would be already detailing someone else to get out there fast. If they lost out on this one, and it certainly looked as if this was a distinct possibility, Eddie would never forgive her, and she wouldn't blame him.

CHAPTER TWO

A SHARP knock on the door brought Sarah out of her musings, and before she could get up to answer the summons the door was flung open and Sean Cartier stood looking down at her half reclining on her bed. 'Surprising what a little hard work can do for you, isn't it?' he said sarcastically. 'Still, by the time the week's up, you'll be hardened. I'm having you moved to the domestic quarters. Mrs Pullman will show you your room when you're through this evening,' he announced, and walked to the door. 'Oh, by the way,' he added conversationally, 'I've had the Press Council on the line. Your editor doesn't let the grass grow under his feet, does he? Unfortunately, owing to the nature of the work, he got nowhere. Just thought you'd like to know,' and he was gone before Sarah could make any kind of response.

'What's up now?' asked Martha, as she entered the room. 'He might have got it in for you, but I don't see why we should all be tarred. He totally ignored me as I passed him,' she complained.

Sarah got up off the bed. 'I'm being shifted to the domestic quarters,' she said, as she started to gather her belongings and stuff them into her overnight case.

'Wow, has he got it in for you!' Martha commented gleefully. 'Well, cheer up. From what was said at the conference, we won't be kept hanging around much longer,' she added, trying to make amends for her earlier remark.

Sarah shrugged lightly, and got on with her packing. She was not going to beg Martha to pass on what news she had been given, and she knew she was just teasing her with titbits. At least she wouldn't have to take any more in that line once she was out of the vicinity.

'The boys' tongues were hanging out after that announcement this morning,' said Martha. 'Of course, I didn't tell them everything. Just said that you'd crossed swords with you know who, and were on the black list,' she added meaningly.

Sarah's brows lifted. Martha wouldn't have been able to resist passing on what Sarah had told her. Only to one or two of them, that was, who would pass on the news to the others. They must have had quite a session in the bar discussing this unusual turn of events, she thought wryly. There was no doubt that some of them would breathe easier now, since they were of the same opinion as Martha was, that she knew more than they did.

'I suppose I'd better write up my notes elsewhere,' Martha said breezily. 'Can't have you peeking, can we?' she added in malicious playfulness.

'Don't bother, I'm just off,' Sarah replied angrily. 'I haven't sunk low enough to pinch anyone's copy yet,' thinking that Martha's copy wouldn't be worth the trouble anyway. Her father would do the work for her when she got back to the newsroom, sorting through the reams of notes she was known to make, relevant or irrelevant.

There was just time for Sarah to take a swift shower before she left for the canteen and her new quarters, and an empty feeling in her stomach reminded her that she hadn't had any lunch at lunchtime. She had been too busy, although Mrs Pullman had put something aside for her when she and Sandy had snatched a quick break, but Sarah had declined the food; she had had a good breakfast before her unannounced interview with Sean Cartier, and the ensuing events had somewhat taken the edge off her appetite—that, and the smell of cooking that pervaded the kitchens.

This time she was more suitably dressed for the work in hand, in trews and light cotton top. Experience had taught her to travel light when packing, but she always had her emergency kit with her where clothes were concerned, and trews had been a must, because she never knew when she would be likely to find herself scrambling over rough terrain in pursuit of a story.

As she left the press quarters and headed towards the canteen, she was still smarting from Martha's uncalled-for innuendo that she would try to sneak a look at her notes, and she only hoped that her comment that a breakthrough was imminent turned out right, even if it did mean having to face her editor with an empty notebook in her hand. There was always the first time, she told herself stoutly, and maybe he would take her past work for the paper into consideration before sacking her!

'Hi! Where's the fire?' called a voice that made Sarah wince in annoyance and look back to see

Charles Ashley striding towards her and gallantly attempting to relieve her of her overnight case, which she resisted firmly. 'Martha says you've stepped on Cartier's corns,' he said breezily. 'Where are you off to now? Been banished to the outer regions, have you?' he asked.

Sarah's lovely eyes showed her annoyance at his flippancy. That wasn't all he knew, she thought. 'I'm off to join the domestics,' she said, managing to keep her voice on an even keel.

'Rotten luck,' he said sympathetically, then paused as if a thought had suddenly struck him. 'Look, why don't we work together on this one? As soon as the whistle's blown, I'll slip you the gen,' he offered innocently. 'No one's to know, are they? I'm of the opinion that Cartier's too big for his boots, and I don't mind putting one over him. What do you say?'

For one second Sarah was tempted, but when she saw the predatory gleam in the *Clarion* reporter's eyes, she gave an abrupt shake of her head. 'Thank you, Charles, but I think not. This is going to be one that got away,' she added, managing to summon up a rueful smile, as she began to walk on.

He caught her arm. 'Look, don't be such a damn fool. This could cost you your job. Lyall's probably chewing nails by now.'

Whatever Sarah would have said, that wouldn't have altered her first refusal, was not uttered, for Sean Cartier had come up behind her. 'You're going to be late for duty, Miss Helm,' he said harshly, giving her a chance to get away.

Before she walked through the canteen entrance, Sarah looked back and saw that Sean was still talking to Charles, and judging from the tight expression on the *Clarion* reporter's face, he was not amused, neither was Sean Cartier.

Sarah's new quarters were not so very different from the room that she had been allotted to share with Martha, but this time she was on her own, and Sarah was not complaining about that. The only other difference was that there was no means of communication. No telecom system to keep the room-mates in touch with the big boss whenever he wished to summon them to a press conference. In other words, Sarah was completely cut off from as much as a whisper of the progress of the project.

By the time she had finished work that evening, she was too tired to care one way or the other. She just wanted peace from the clatter of cooking pan lids, steam, and the general hubbub of a frantically busy kitchen.

On the one low table in her room sat a tray with a covered dish, to keep the supper Mrs Pullman had insisted she took to her room, for she had noticed that Sarah had only grabbed a sandwich to keep her going during her working hours, and she didn't want what was turning out to be an extremely reliable worker collapsing at the sink through lack of sustenance.

Sarah didn't want that either, but somehow the thought of food was repellent to her, and she would have preferred a plate of sandwiches, in fact, anything that wasn't cooked.

After one or two jabs at the now congealing lamb stew, Sarah gave it best, and took a shower, which somewhat revived her, then, not bothering to dress again in her day clothes, she slipped on her nightdress and dressing gown, since she might as well be comfortable as she wasn't going anywhere, she thought, as she stretched out on her cot bed and considered her future.

A future that didn't look too bright at this point in time. Charles Ashley had hit the nail on the head when he had pointed out that she could lose her job. Sarah's smooth brow creased, and her eyes narrowed. There wasn't anything she could do about it. She would lose her job. Of all the bad luck, she thought miserably, that she should have been given this assignment. There was another reporter who could have covered it, and he was a bit more familiar with the scientific terms used on such projects, but no, Eddie Lyall had elected to keep Eric Morris kicking his heels around the office waiting for any sudden story that might crop up, and sent Sarah instead.

Eric would now be on standby, she thought, ready to take off at a moment's notice, then she shook her head, making a golden curl fall over her right eyebrow. If she knew anything about her boss, Eric Morris would be in Darwin, with their editor burning up the telegraph lines to keep him informed and ready to make his debut at the site at the first given opportunity.

Not that Sarah could see any such opportunity occurring. If anyone meant what they said, Sean Cartier did; he wasn't the type to change his mind. She drew in a deep breath. Never in her wildest dreams had she imagined that such a situation might arise, where she would meet someone who not only knew Don but was actually related to him. She had moved on from the small paper she used to work for and was now at the top of her profession, based in Sydney, and although the paper was privately owned, it was one of the city's most respected journals.

Or had been, she thought with a twist of her soft lips, until Sean Cartier had come on the scene. Sarah's thoughts roamed on. Sean Cartier had not known of her connection with Don when she had first arrived with her fellow reporters, and that meant that someone had made a point of passing on the news to him.

Her mind ran over the present company. Martha? She shook her head. Martha couldn't have kept such a juicy story to herself, not when it concerned Sarah; besides, she wasn't clever enough to fool Sarah with her assumed surprise.

One by one, Sarah discounted the others, and that left two still on her list. One was Jim Rokeby, about the oldest of the journalists there, who might conceivably have stored away a few facts in his analytical brain, and had once accused her of trading on her looks to get a scoop on a story they were covering.

Finally she crossed him off the list too. There was an unwritten code among them, and personal worries, tragedies, call it what you like, were never aired in public. Whatever snippets were picked up in the course of their work were never impinged upon. As odd as it seemed, although their work entailed ferreting out news about people in the news, their private lives remained private, and that left only one on her list, and that was Charles Ashley.

Sarah pushed back the curl with a weary action. Why on earth should Charles wish to queer her pitch? If anything he had more reason than the others to smooth her path along, hoping for certain benefits to fall his way.

Suddenly Sarah sat up. What a ninny she was! Of course it was Charles! He was the only one interested enough in her private life to obtain background data about her—and to think she'd almost fallen for it! she thought angrily. What a snake he was! Sean Cartier had got a bit too interested in her for Charles's liking, and he hadn't been able to take it. Charles's prowess with the opposite sex was a well-known fact. Women fell over themselves to curry his favours. If anyone used their looks to further their career, then Charles Ashley did, she thought scathingly, and he wasn't too fussy how he got the story either. By the time the ink was dry on the presses, he had lost interest in whoever he had been paying court to, to gain access to the inside story.

Her slim hands clenched on the plain counterpane beneath her. If she got the chance she would take him up on his offer of filling her in with the news. One rotten turn deserves another, she told herself savagely, and just wait until he tried to collect—would she give him a few home truths!

Sarah's eyes fell on her overnight case with her silk suit still stuffed away inside it. She ought to hang it up, she thought absentmindedly. With any luck it shouldn't be long before she could put it on again and get back to civilisation, whatever that held for her now.

After she had put her suit away, she sat on her

bed and studied the amount of information she had managed to get so far on the project. It didn't amount to much, and after a while the silence got through to her. She knew that Mrs Pullman, and Sandy, her niece, shared the small chalet with her, and presumed that they had elected to spend the evening in the social club, a small shack across the way that served as an entertainment area for the drillers and maintenance crew. Mrs Pullman had mentioned it to Sarah during the day, and Sandy, still a little in awe of Sarah, had shyly urged her to 'come along' and said that they were a well disciplined crew. Not that Sarah had thought they could be anything else, not with a man like Sean Cartier in charge of the project!

As this thought occurred to her, so did another one, and her eyes narrowed. If she was the bright reporter that everyone apparently thought she was, she ought to join them. There was a lot that she could pick up from scraps of conversation from the men who wouldn't be on their guard, although she wouldn't put it past Cartier not to make a point of warning them to watch out for her.

She sighed. It wouldn't be necessary. Even if she got anything, she couldn't pass it on. There was no hope of smuggling anything out, not unless Charles Ashley followed through on his offer, and somehow, after that conversation he had had with Cartier, during which he would have been warned off, Sarah was certain, she couldn't see him risking it. He wouldn't put his own job in jeopardy, because that was what it would amount to if he was slung off the site.

At this point of her calculations there was a perfunctory knock at her door, and as before, Sean Cartier was in the room before she could answer the summons.

The fact that she was in her dressing gown, a caftan affair of glossy silk, too fancy really for such an assignment but ideal because of its featherlight weight, did not cause him a moment's embarrassment, Sarah noted, as her indignant eyes met his bland ones.

'I might have been undressing!' she exclaimed angrily. 'Next time, please wait until I ask you to come in,' she added crisply.

His eyes swept briefly over her slight figure, and his voice was insolent as he replied. 'You're in my territory now. I keep politeness for ladies of my acquaintance—and I don't count the press, and certainly not you, among them.'

Sarah's wide eyes and angry flush acknowledged this pointed remark. He hadn't actually said 'the gutter press', but he had implied it all the same. 'Get out!' she snapped furiously. 'I don't have to put up with this. You've got me off the story. I'm paying for my keep, and that's as far as it goes! I've no option but to accept your ruling, but I'm not standing for any more insults from you. Just go away!' she added angrily, as she swept to the door and opened it wide, showing him that she meant what she said.

Some people, Sarah discovered, were hard to convince, and Sean Cartier was one of them, for she found herself unceremoniously flung away from the door, and correcting her balance, saw him close it with a slam that must have echoed down the corridor of the chalet, and probably across half the yard.

If he was in a temper then he had himself well in hand, for when he spoke again it was in a smooth, almost caressing voice that Sarah didn't care for at all. 'Acting the lady will get you nowhere,' he said blandly. 'It might fool the others, in fact it did fool me before I found out a few facts about you. How many other poor devils have you driven off the edge?' he asked harshly. 'No wonder you've got to the top of your profession! I can guess how you got your stories. Men are so gullible when they're off their guard, aren't they? The next thing the poor devils know is that they're headline news—pillow talk reported in double space on the front page!'

Sarah wanted to shake her head to clear the fog that had descended around her. She didn't believe any of this. The only thing that did make sense was the fact that it had been Charles Ashley who had put her in this mess. It was just the sort of wording he would have used, it was the way that he collected his data, and was all the confirmation that Sarah had needed. Her hands gripped the silk folds of her dressing gown at her side. There was nothing she could say in her defence. He had obviously believed everything that Charles had told him, and there was nothing that she could do about it, then or later.

'Stumped for once?' he drawled, then as Sarah turned away from him to show him that there was no point in going on with the conversation, he went on, 'Your editor was on the line again this afternoon. He sounded desperate,' he said conversationally. 'I suppose, like everyone else, they have their job to think about too, someone waiting on the sidelines to take over, I suppose.'

Sarah looked at him. He knew something, she thought, and wondered how much. Eddie didn't get on with the paper's proprietor, a prissy, mean man, who constantly preached to his staff on upholding the paper's tradition for honest reporting, but was not above running a private vendetta against someone who had stepped on his toes in the commercial world. It was definitely a case of 'do what I say, but not what I do', with Marchmont Willis.

Only the paper's popularity had kept Eddie at his post—that, and his strict observance of the rules as laid down by his irascible boss. Rules that had at times to be quoted to the self-same boss, and that had infuriated him beyond measure. All this Sarah knew; she also knew that this was not general knowledge, and wondered who his informant had been, for this was nothing to do with Charles Ashley. Charles had only been concerned with railroading her into a compromising position, he wouldn't have bothered to relate the inner machinations of the paper's staff, even if he had known about it.

Sean Cartier had also been right about the 'someone waiting on the sidelines'. 'Oily Oliver', as the staff named him behind his back, was the sub-editor, and a crony of Marchmont Willis. A yes-man if there ever was one, and there would be several heads that would roll should he ever take over from Eddie. It was well known that he had a hit list, and Sarah wasn't sure if she too wasn't on that list. She had certainly not gone out of her way to gain his favour, and there had been a time when she had first joined the staff—she sighed inwardly; what was the point of worrying about that now? She'd lost her job anyway.

'Wondering how much I know?' Sean asked silkily, making Sarah want to hit him. He had a nasty habit of correctly picking up her thoughts. 'Well, that's my secret. I happen to know a lot about the *Daily*. Trouble is, I admire Eddie Lyall. He used to cover a lot of these assignments in the early days, and he's straight. It's not his fault that his star reporter is a tramp, is it?' His firm lips twisted as he shot Sarah a look of dislike. 'So we shall have to compromise, won't we?'

Sarah's eyes were wary as she met his hard gaze. Not for nothing, of course, she thought angrily, and she had a good idea of what he had in mind. He was attracted to her, she knew this without a doubt, otherwise he would have thrown her off the site instead of electing to play this cat-and-mouse game with her. Her soft lips clamped together as she waited for the pay-off line, and thinking how much she was going to enjoy telling him to get lost. Whatever attraction she had felt for him—and she had been strongly attracted at the start of their acquaintance, she couldn't deny—had now gone. She would prefer a wrestling match with Charles, rather than have to put up with this hateful character, she told herself.

Sean's blue eyes studied her and seemed to sear right through her, and for once she didn't mind if he could read her thoughts. At least he would know the answer to the proposition she was sure that he had in mind. 'No, not that,' he said curtly. 'I'll admit I was interested, in fact, more than interested—but then you'd know that, wouldn't you?' His eyes narrowed. 'There's nothing like the truth to cure that sort of madness, so if you're hoping to cash in on the romantic stakes, I'm afraid you've got a shock coming. The plain fact is that I've had second thoughts. I don't see why Eddie Lyall should be penalised. I've nothing against the paper, only its star reporter. So, in return for my co-operation, you stay on at the camp. Mrs Pullman tells me that you've proved a good worker. We've more men moving in soon, and we'll need the extra help. I want to keep the staff down to a minimum because of the security risks, as I'm sure you'll appreciate,' he added casually.

'And what explanation will you give my editor?' Sarah demanded sarcastically, just to keep the conversation going. She had no intention of complying with this stipulation. When the others left, she was going, too, and woe betide anyone who tried to stop her!

'You can use your imagination on that, surely?' he replied smoothly. 'You won't be the only girl who suddenly decides she's had enough of the city life and wants to settle down to being a plain old housewife, having found the right man, of course,' he added blandly.

Sarah gasped at his audacity. 'If you think Eddie will swallow that, I advise you to think again,' she replied waspishly. 'It's ridiculous,

even if——' she swallowed, hating the deep flush
she could feel rising in her cheeks. 'Even if it
were true,' she went on determinedly, 'I would
have to go back to Sydney. I share a flat with two
girls, and they need my contribution to the rent.'
She smiled sweetly at him. 'Sorry, but it's not on.
It was a good try, though. As for losing out on
the story—well, we'll see about that. There are
other sources, you know, and I'd rather take pot
luck on losing my job than stay here a day longer
than necessary. When the rest go, I go, and that's
final!' she flung at him.

Sean's blue eyes studied her, taking in her
lovely sapphire blue eyes, now brilliant with
temper, and he gave an exaggerated sigh. 'What a
pity,' he drawled, and shook his head. 'I really
could have gone for you. As the feline species
goes, you're magnificent, and believe me, I'm a
good judge, but it's underneath that counts, isn't
it, and all I can see now is a cheap little go-getter
who happens to be good at her job. A job,
incidentally, that she doesn't have now.' His eyes
glinted like blue icicles. 'Thanks for putting me
in the picture about the flat. I'll mention it to
Eddie while I'm on the line and get him to pass
on the news to your pals to look for another
flatmate. I'll settle for the rest of the month, of
course,' he declared magnanimously, giving
Sarah a wolfish grin.

Sarah heard, but she didn't believe it. He
couldn't force her to stay, and he was living in a
fool's paradise if he thought he could bully her
into accepting his dictates. 'I said I was going
when the others go,' she replied, forcing herself

to stay calm, since she was now certain that she was dealing with someone who appeared to have lost all sense of reason.

Sean's grin widened as he glanced at his watch. 'I'm afraid you're two hours too late,' he told her. 'They won't get in until the evening, so your editor will be the first to get the news, plus a few more details that were not given out for general release, but enough to keep him interested for further developments. He knows enough about this type of work to keep him happy on that score. I feel very kindly disposed towards Eddie Lyall for giving me the opportunity of catching up with you. Don wasn't a good correspondent, and I hadn't much to go on. When I heard the news of his death, I was out on a site the other side of the country, and out of circulation for months. By the time I arrived on the scene, you'd taken off, and it was no wonder.' His voice hardened. 'Unfortunately, the law doesn't cover your sort of crime, and you got away with it scot free, but not this time.'

Sarah had stopped listening when he had said that the others had gone. Her mind was on other things, such as how she was going to get off the site. To her way of thinking, this was of paramount importance. There was an air-strip somewhere at the back of the camp for the plane that brought in supplies, and somehow she would have to work out a plan to smuggle herself aboard on one of those trips.

She looked across at the man facing her, standing with arms across his powerful chest and surveying her as if she were an interesting

specimen he had just added to his collection,
which prompted her to remark caustically, 'I'm
afraid you've picked on the wrong person. I'm
not a bit intimidated by your scheme for
revenge—I suppose that's what it amounts to,
doesn't it?—and you're wasting your time if you
think you can coerce me into accepting your
proposition. I like my editor, too, but there are
limits, and this is one of them. When he hears
about this ridiculous vendetta you've embarked
upon, I wouldn't be surprised if I keep my job
after all,' she added, feeling confidence creeping
back into her voice.

A confidence, however, that proved to be
slightly misplaced by Sean's tight-lipped reply.
'How much do you know about Eddie's private
life?' he asked, and at Sarah's surprised blink at
this, he went on, 'I suppose being a reporter
hardens you to other people's troubles, doesn't it?
When some poor devil hits the headlines, it's all
grist to the mill, isn't it? Just good copy to add to
the list of the star reporter's ego!'

Sarah did not bother to challenge this. She
would be wasting her breath. If he knew so much
about her paper, he would also know that it was a
reputable paper that reported the facts without
embellishment; the other publications could be
relied upon to dot the i's and cross the t's.
Intelligent people could read between the lines,
and didn't need a blueprint.

'Just in case, you didn't know,' Sean went on
smoothly, 'Eddie needs his job—more than most,
as it happens. I'll give you the benefit of the
doubt that you don't know his circumstances.

Like your affair with Don, it's not something that he would want noised abroad. His son's in a classy nursing home. He's a drug addict, or was. The treatment he's getting is the best that can be had. When they're cured, they stay cured, but it's expensive, and I don't think it leaves Eddie a lot over to play with, if you see what I mean,' he added meaningly.

Sarah's first reaction was that this was the nearest approach to blackmail that she had ever encountered. Even if it were true, it was a pretty rotten way to make her toe the line just to satisfy a personal grudge of his against her. She wasn't inclined to give in quite so easily as all that. Her blue eyes met his defiantly. 'If we lose our jobs,' she said, reminding him that they were only discussing possibilities, for Eddie, anyway, she thought, if not for her, 'perhaps we could start a paper between us. Eddie's not all that happy where he is.'

'I think that's a non-starter, don't you?' Sean said hatefully. 'I can't see a rich backer laying out good money on such a scheme on a pair who'd fallen down on a story as big as this one.'

Sarah's eyes glinted back at him, openly showing her dislike of the man. So they had hit the jackpot, and it must have been a big strike. Her gaze left him, and centred on the door behind him. She was expected to cave in now, but there had to be another way out. Her small teeth caught her lower lip. He had said something about giving Eddie extra information that the others hadn't got. If she could only find out what that was, she would have a good excuse for late reporting. Why didn't she go along with this detestable man's proposition? If she played her cards right, she could still keep her job. It meant staying on at the camp, of course, but not for long. The wet was due in about three weeks' time, and that would be the end of the project for that season anyway. She could tell Eddie that she was taking three weeks' holiday, couldn't she? He would be only too relieved that he had the story, and he wouldn't crib too much.

'So, as I was saying,' Sean broke into her musings, 'Eddie's in no position to chance his arm on any wildcat schemes that might or might not come off.'

Sarah's eyes gave nothing of her thoughts away, but her voice was not quite so belligerent as it had been before, as she said abruptly, 'So?'

Sean nodded, accepting this as her acceptance of his terms. 'So Eddie's given the data. Plus a hint of a bigger find to keep him happy and not fret about the loss of his star reporter.' He acknowledged the dangerous glint in Sarah's eyes as he prodded her with his sneering opinion of her hard-earned reputation. 'I'll keep my word. It all depends on your co-operation.'

Sarah gave an impatient nod of the head. 'What exactly is this other find?' she asked abruptly.

Sean's firm lips twisted into a sneer. 'Once a newshound, always a newshound, eh? Well, I suppose there's no harm in giving you some of the data. You're not going to be able to use it. Even if you hadn't accepted my terms, I didn't intend to let you off the hook for quite some time.'

CHAPTER THREE

WHAT little information Sean did give Sarah was enough to prove that her editor would be more than satisfied with the turn of events, even if it was at Sarah's expense.

The 'C' factor, a rare and commercially sought-after power-releasing mineral, had been found on the site, but only the oil find had been made public—or would be, when the news was proclaimed in the press the following day, and even if the more astute members of the press fraternity suspected a cover-up, there was nothing that they could do about it but accept Sean Cartier's ruling that they quit the site.

Sarah pondered on this as soon as Sean Cartier left her to fulfil his part of the bargain, as he had put it, to keep Sarah's editor in the picture.

What exactly he would say about her continued absence, Sarah had no idea, but she was of the opinion that he would hint that she was still covering the story; determined as he was to carry out what he considered a fitting punishment for her callous treatment of his cousin, he must have realised that Eddie would never swallow the story about her chucking up her job and deciding to settle down. He would have to do better than that, she thought angrily, unless he wanted to find himself had up on an abduction charge, which was what it amounted to anyway, she told herself grimly.

No one, but no one, could take the law into his own hands like that. He might be king of that small domain, but just wait until she got back to Sydney! She recalled the raillery she had had to put up with after Sean Cartier had singled her out for attention soon after they had got to the site. Remarks such as 'was she dangling after a rich husband?' and if so, she had 'struck the jackpot'.

Her small chin jutted out. If that were true, then she wouldn't need a job. She would sue Mr High and Mighty for all she could get. Her blue eyes narrowed in speculation. Why, she could even back another paper! The kind of paper Eddie had talked about producing when in the middle of another set-to with the proprietor. It was every editor's dream to print precisely what he wanted to print, with no holds barred because of commercial interests.

Sarah sighed. It was all very well making plans, but first she had to get out of the place—a place as well guarded as Fort Knox, and for the life of her she didn't see how. Her first thought about the airstrip was a non-runner. It was at the back of the site, and the wire fencing that enclosed the area also surrounded the airstrip, and there was always someone posted on the gates, during the day anyway, as there were no night flights, and even if Sarah did manage to get out during the dead of night, there was nowhere for her to hide in the flat expanse of desert territory while she waited for a plane to arrive. It just wasn't on.

After accepting this salient fact, she consoled herself with the thought that three weeks was not

a lifetime. Thank goodness for the wet! At least
that could be relied upon to bring the project to a
halt, and surely she could put up with the
situation that long, couldn't she? She sighed. She
didn't have much choice in the matter anyway.

It did, of course, give her time to work out her
next move when she got to Sydney, and which
lawyer was going to receive her instructions, so
she would have something to keep her amused,
she thought, but instead of cheering her, this
thought depressed her. It was not what she had
wanted. It would mean a lot of things coming
out, things that were better left as they were, and
for a brief moment, Sarah's mind went back over
the past, particularly to that squalid little flat and
its occupants, that had been the start of
everything.

If Sean Cartier had any sense he would settle
out of court, she thought. In spite of his
prejudice against her and the press in general, she
couldn't see him giving them a field day, so she
had the upper hand, didn't she?

Somewhat cheered by this thought, Sarah went
back to considering her plans for escape. She did
so want to spike his guns by getting away. Not
that she would be irresponsible enough to
proclaim the latest discovery; if there had been a
clamp-down on it, there would be good reasons
for the clamp-down, and Sarah wanted to
continue with her career. Not that Sean Cartier
would know this, he hadn't given her the benefit
of the doubt on anything so far, only when it
suited him, she thought grimly, as she recalled
what had been said about Eddie Lyall's personal

life. So—if she accomplished nothing else, she would certainly give him a few bad moments, and that was worth something!

The following day Sarah was back at her post at the kitchen sink. Her legs and back had slowly recovered from the shock of physical exhaustion, and buoyed up by her inner calculations of how much all this was going to cost Sean Cartier, she worked cheerfully at her task.

That evening, she had told herself, she would take up Mrs Pullman's invitation and join them in the social hut; there just might be a glimmer of an idea to be found there concerning her cherished hope of an escape route, and she wasn't going to find it sitting in her room all evening.

By lunch time, however, she was given something else to think about, for a depressed-looking Mrs Pullman sought her out with, 'I knew it was too good to last! Mr Cartier's putting you on other work. He wants to see you in his office after lunch.' She frowned in annoyance. 'I'll miss you. I don't suppose that gormless lad from the laundry that they're sending to replace you will be half as useful.'

Sarah murmured something on the lines that she was sorry, too, just as she was getting used to the work, etc., but inside she was seething. So he was going to send her to the laundry, was he? Well, that was going to cost him a few more thousands when she sued him, she thought grimly.

Shortly after two, she presented herself at Sean's office. She could have been sent straight to the laundry, couldn't she? she thought angrily, as she tapped on the office door and awaited the summons to enter his august presence—but no, he wanted to enjoy seeing her discomfiture on learning her new position, and no matter what, she wasn't going to allow him that satisfaction, she told herself firmly.

'Ah, there you are!' Sean Cartier said breezily, as Sarah entered the office, as if she had just been passing by and he had caught her attention. He pointed to the seat in front of his desk.

Sarah glared at him, but stayed right where she was. She would rather take it standing up like a man, she thought. It shouldn't take long.

'Sit down!' he commanded. 'You're going to need a seat in a minute,' he added in an amused tone, and thrust a piece of paper which had the print-out of a cablegram on it.

Sarah took the piece of paper and perused its contents. It was addressed to her, which under the circumstances was surprising enough, but the message it contained was even more perplexing. 'Congratulations. You did a good job. We'll miss you. Eddie.'

This, then, was the result of Sean Cartier's telephone conversation with her editor, but the wording was odd to say the least, and her eyes left the cablegram and rested on Sean. 'Am I supposed to know what this means?' she asked.

He grinned back at her, his white teeth gleaming against his tanned features. 'It means that as of this moment, you are no longer employed by the *Daily*,' he said pompously.

Sarah's eyes glinted dangerously. 'On whose say-so?' she asked quietly.

'On my say-so,' Sean replied smoothly.

A very nasty idea was forming in Sarah's mind about this time, for suddenly the word 'congratulations' floated in front of her eyes in double-spaced capitals, and there was only one reason why Eddie would have put that—she swallowed. He couldn't have gone through with that crazy idea of his, could he? She almost shook her head. Eddie wasn't born yesterday; he'd never wear that. She looked back at the man sitting in front of her, and who had never taken his eyes off her. She had to know. 'Why the congratulations?' she asked.

'Can't you guess?' he replied, the smile now definitely wolfish. 'I think I did mention what I had in mind.'

Sarah's cheeks flamed in pure temper. So he had told that stupid story! 'Of all the ridiculous ideas!' she fumed at him. 'I gave you more credit than that.' She flung the cablegram back at him. 'And I give Eddie more credit than to believe it. Is that all you wanted to see me about?' she demanded. 'I understand I'm being taken off kitchen duties. No doubt you've some other delightful work lined up for me,' she added pithily.

Sean continued to study her. 'I like you in a temper,' he said softly. 'It brings out the wildcat in you. I'm going to enjoy bringing you down to earth—you've got too exalted an opinion of yourself. All those admirers have gone to your head. Still, all that's changed from now on. You're right about the new job,' he added airily. 'I can't have my fiancée doing menial work, can I?'

Sarah stared at him. That wasn't the only thing she had been right about, she thought. He had lost his senses!

His eyes mocked her. 'I think you'd better sit down before you fall down,' he suggested silkily. 'Yes, I did say fiancée. As you so rightly pointed out, your editor wouldn't have accepted a vague reference of you settling down; I had to make it more plausible. I told him that no future wife of mine would be expected to earn her living—also,' he paused, and his eyes narrowed as they met Sarah's wide stare, 'that I wouldn't hear of your going back without me.' He gave a mirthless smile. 'I guess your editor's just an old softie underneath that hard exterior. Said he'd known it would happen one day, and asked for an invitation to the wedding.'

Sarah did sit. Her legs did not seem able to carry her weight. She wanted to shout and scream at this man, who looked sane enough, but must be mad, shouting wouldn't get her anywhere, she thought dully, it would only give him more cause to hit out at her. Her only hope was in playing the game his way until she could get away.

At that moment the telephone on the desk rang, and Sean frowned at the instrument that dared to interrupt his enjoyment of watching the different emotions that ran the whole gamut from disbelief to resigned weariness on Sarah's face. His abrupt 'Yes,' as he picked the phone up said it all. 'Well, send someone out there,' he barked out authoritatively, 'and then get on to the coach firm and give them a rocket. We've got more to

do than pander to their incompetence!' He
slammed the phone down and transferred his
annoyance to Sarah. 'That will be one of your
jobs now,' he said tersely. 'You're the official
press secretary for the site from now on. You'll
also deal with any other enquiry that comes in—
apart, that is, from the actual work on the site;
that's my province, and you'd be wise to
remember that. No snooping around—got that?'
he added harshly.

Sarah took a deep breath. She couldn't see a
great deal of work coming her way under those
stipulations, but it was better than nothing. At
least she would be in contact with the outside
world. As for the other position he had landed
her in—well, she didn't want to go too deeply
into that.

Her silence was taken as acceptance, and if he
was disappointed by her non-reaction, he did not
show it as he jerked his desk drawer open and all
but threw a notebook at Sarah. 'You can make a
note to charge time and a half to Sunset Tours
for the use of a site tractor. A damn fool driver's
got stuck in a rut a mile away from camp. They
know full well they have to take it easy along that
route, but they're always trying to beat time.'

Sarah duly made a note in the book, then
looked up at him. 'Aren't you trying to beat time,
too?' she asked, and at Sean's raised brows, went
on, 'the wet won't be long, will it?'

His blue eyes studied her. 'So that's what
you've got in mind, is it?' he said. 'Counting on a
three-week drudge, are you? No wonder you took
it so well! I'm afraid I've got a nasty surprise in

store for you. Sure, we stop excavating for the time being, but that's when the real work is done. Paper work, I'm talking about, and we've enough to work on to keep us busy for quite some time.' He gave her another wolfish grin. 'You'll be well up on scientific data by the time the site starts operating again. For once, my reports won't be handwritten.' His grin widened. 'You know, I could make a good case out of keeping you on as my personal assistant. You haven't got a job, have you?'

Sarah's fingers clutching the notebook stiffened. She said nothing, but her eyes spoke volumes.

Sean nodded complacently. 'Not to your liking, eh? Well, that's to be expected. It's a bit of a come-down from your usual work. No more cosy dinners with intended victims, no more chat-ups in intimate surroundings. The only male in your vicinity will be someone who's wise to you. I'm willing to be entertained, of course,' his firm lips twisted disdainfully, 'but that's as far as it's going.' His blue, ice-cold eyes met hers. 'There'll be times, no doubt, when you'll think you've made a conquest, but I'm telling you now, there'll be nothing you can rely on, not from one day to the next,' he added grimly.

Sarah's flush deepened, and her eyes flashed back at him. 'If you mean what I think you mean,' she said, hardly able to keep her voice on an even keel, she was so angry. 'You're living in a fool's paradise to even consider that I'd——' she stopped, lost for words.

Sean's expressive brows lifted. 'Make a play for

me?' he finished for her, and nodded grimly. 'Sure you will. You're no different from the rest of your tribe. You couldn't resist it! Besides, I'm considered a good catch—or hadn't you heard that?' he jeered at her.

Sarah was beyond replying. All she could think of was that she was stuck there for goodness knew how long. The work could go on for months, and if that wasn't bad enough, she was going to have to put up with this despicable character. She would have preferred the canteen work, and was tempted to ask to be kept on there, but decided not to make a point of it. He would enjoy turning the request down.

'You can go back to your old quarters,' he went on. 'That way I can keep in touch with you. You can use the next room as an office—I'll get it fixed up while you sort through these notes of mine.' He thrust a bulky file at her. 'I hope you can read my writing. In any case, you've got plenty of time to study, haven't you?' he added hatefully, and got up and walked to the door. 'Thank you for reminding me about the wet. I'll have a word with Mrs Pullman to make sure we've got enough supplies to keep us going if it gets really bad.'

As the door slammed behind him, Sarah sat staring at the file in her hands, and after a brief glance through its contents, slammed it down on the desk. This was ridiculous! she thought angrily. She knew nothing about that kind of work, and what was more, she didn't want to know! Half her time would be spent in asking questions, and it just wasn't on!

Her angry glance rested on the telephone on Sean's desk, and her eyes narrowed as a thought occurred to her. The next moment she had picked the receiver up and was immediately connected with an unseen source on the site that answered with a flat 'Yes?'

Sarah immediately asked for an outside line. 'Sorry, miss, only Mr Cartier can make outside calls,' replied the disembodied voice.

Sarah took a deep breath. This was her only chance to contact the outside world, and she didn't intend to lose it. 'Look, I'm Sarah Helm. Mr Cartier has just appointed me as the site press secretary. I want to place a call to the *Daily*, Sydney office,' she ordered in a no-nonsense voice, hoping to intimidate the operator, but the hand holding the receiver trembled slightly as she thought she heard Sean Cartier returning.

'Sorry about that,' came the laconic reply. 'You'll still have to check with Mr Cartier. He didn't say anything about anyone else making outside calls. If you'd get Mr Cartier to——'

That was as far as Sarah allowed him to get before slamming the phone down in frustrated fury. So far everything was going his way. He'd sewn things up pretty tightly, she thought, but there had to be a way out of her dilemma, and by hook or by crook, she was going to find it. She wasn't beaten yet!

She was still standing by the desk when Sean returned.

'That's all right, then,' he said in a satisfied voice that made Sarah want to scream. 'You'd better go and collect your gear,' he ordered, and picked up the file she had thrown back on to the desk. 'You can do some studying while the other room's being seen to,' and he thrust the file at her.

Sarah glared at him, but she had no choice but to accept the work. 'Talking of gear,' she said, 'I'd like to know just how long I'm to be kept here. As you can imagine, I didn't come prepared for a long stay.' She took a deep breath, as she saw Sean's white teeth gleam in a wicked smile. 'Apart from what I'm wearing,' she went on determinedly, 'I have only one other change of clothes. I don't suppose you thought of that, did you?' she challenged him angrily.

Sean's firm mouth twisted wryly. 'No, I guess I didn't,' he replied smoothly. 'I'll have to get you fixed up with something. Mrs Pullman's too big, and her niece is a bit on the small side,' he mused, to Sarah's fury. 'You're about size twelve, aren't you? Still, if Mrs Pullman can spare a couple of dresses, you can wrap them round you, can't you?'

'I'm not wearing anything of Mrs Pullman's or anyone else's clothes!' Sarah spat out at him.

With the speed of lightning Sean moved towards her, and she found her wrist caught in a vicelike hold. 'You don't seem to have got the hang of things yet,' he said harshly. 'Count yourself damn lucky that you're not in jail! As I've said, the law can't prosecute you for your type of crime, but that's not good enough for me. If I can save some other poor devil from falling into your clutches, then it will be a worthwhile exercise. In fact,' he added grimly, 'I'm quite looking forward to it. Things can get pretty dull out here during the off season,' he added meaningly.

'I only hope,' Sarah ground out furiously, 'that you're as rich as it's rumoured you are. When I'm finished with you, you're going to need a job—any job!' she added wildly, 'because I'm going to sue you for all you've got!'

The hold on her wrist tightened even further, making her wince in pain, but she was too angry to let it sidetrack her, and she didn't show any fear when Sean jerked her against his hard body and held her in a suffocating embrace with his face only inches away from hers. 'And when I'm finished with you,' he grated in a low menacing voice, 'you'll be on your knees begging me to marry you!' He flung her away from him, walked round the desk to his chair, and sat down. 'So— now we've got the air cleared,' he said, in a conversational voice, as if he were discussing the weather, 'you can get down to work. The typewriter should be set up by now. Just save any queries for this evening. We can go over them during dinner,' he added pompously.

'I'm not having dinner with you!' Sarah said acidly. 'I'd rather eat in the canteen with the men.'

He studied her briefly before saying softly, 'That's just not on. You play the game my way. You either dine with me, or not at all. Apart from getting awfully hungry, you're going to get very lonely stuck in that room of yours. Of course, I could have the dinner served there, but it's much more comfortable in my quarters, isn't it?' he added smoothly.

For the first time in her life Sarah seriously considered homicide! Surely under the circumstances, she would get a light sentence, if not complete acquittal!

Her mind was fully occupied in carrying out her cherished scheme of eliminating her tormentor, as she made her way back to the quarters she had shared with Mrs Pullman and her niece, and as she passed the canteen entrance, she noticed a van drawn up outside. It caught her eye because it was not a site vehicle, and glancing at the name on the van painted in eye-catching bright blue and white stripes, she saw that it belonged to the National Park.

Sarah stood and looked at it for a second or two, then she went in to the canteen to find Mrs Pullman, who was at that moment engaged in signing a delivery sheet for a tall, gangly-looking man, dressed in a rather grimy sweatshirt and faded denim shorts, and going by the cap on his head which bore the same name as that on the van, was obviously the driver, and had just delivered a box of huge delicious-looking pineapples. 'Same next week?' the driver asked, as he picked up the signed delivery note, and at Mrs Pullman's nod of confirmation, went on his way.

Mrs Pullman then caught sight of Sarah, whose mind was now seething with possibilities as to how she could get out of the site. She hadn't known about this delivery from the National Park, and had assumed that all the supplies had come by plane from Darwin. This, then, was where the fresh fruit came from.

'Mr Cartier changed his mind?' Mrs Pullman

asked hopefully, as she turned her attention to Sarah.

'I'm afraid not,' Sarah said. 'I'm on my way to get my things. I'm back at the main section where I was before,' and seeing Mrs Pullman's obvious disappointment at the news, she hurried on with, 'I didn't know the fruit came from the National Park. I thought everything came from Darwin.'

'So it does,' Mrs Pullman replied. 'Well, nearly everything, but we had some bad weather a while ago when the plane was grounded, and the Park helped us out.' She nodded towards the box of pineapples. 'We never got such beauts as those, though, and they go a lot further than the others, so Mr Cartier agreed to make it a standing order.'

Sarah was tempted to ask whether the delivery came on the same day each week, but decided not to push the matter. She knew that Mrs Pullman was curious about her, but was certain that she had no idea that Sarah was being detained against her will. She would know that Sean Cartier had singled Sarah out for his personal attention when she had arrived at the site. You couldn't keep that sort of thing quiet, not in an enclosed area like that. Everything the big boss did was common gossip. They hadn't much else to occupy their time with.

What would make sense to Mrs Pullman was the fact that Sarah was chasing the boss, and had stayed on in the hope of making it a permanent attachment. This thought did nothing for Sarah's ego, but she knew that this sort of thing was a fact of life, particularly where money was concerned, and Sean Cartier was wealthy. He was also good-looking, and knew it, she thought scathingly, and judging from what Martha had told her about a friend of hers, a playboy where women were concerned.

After a few more mundane remarks, Sarah left Mrs Pullman to get on with her work, and went to the chalet to pick up her kit, which did not take her long. She had little enough to pack, and at the thought of Sean Cartier's threat of providing her with one or two of Mrs Pullman's dresses, she very nearly broke her stern resolution not to let things get her down, and fought back the compelling need to have a good howl.

A few moments later she left the chalet, clutching her overnight bag in one hand and Sean Cartier's file in the other, that she had found herself still carrying long after she had left his office. It just went to show what a state she was in, she thought angrily. It only took a few minutes of his company to completely rout her normally calm presence of mind. She would end up a raving idiot, given time, if she had to put up with him for long, of that she was certain.

There was, of course, the fact that if she had taken the file to her old quarters first, which normally she would have done, instead of carting it around with her, she would not have seen the Park van outside the canteen, for the delivery had not taken long, so perhaps for once fate was on her side, she mused, as she entered the long passage of the main building that led to the room she had shared with Martha. On entering the room, she wrinkled her nose as the smell of stale cosmetics that still hung in the air assailed her, and glanced up at the air extractor on the ceiling, that was apparently still in working order, with its fan whirling monotonously round. The windows were there to give light only, and were never opened, for there were no nets for protection against the various flying insects that would home in as if guided by radar.

Sarah's glance moved on and rested on the intercom speaker, from which numerous summons would undoubtedly come in the not so distant future, and she wished that there was some way that she could cut the connection. This of course was only wishful thinking. If she didn't answer the summons, Sean would only stalk down to her room and yank her out, and there was no sense in asking for more trouble.

As she felt despondency edging nearer, Sarah forced herself to concentrate on positive thinking. Today was Thursday, and that meant that the next fruit delivery would come next Thursday, and somehow she had to be in the area around three-thirty. Better make it three o'clock, she thought, to be on the safe side. She could hang around inside the canteen entrance, there was a small enclosure there where the dustbins were kept out of sight until they could be collected and which would be ideal for Sarah's purpose, since the refuse was only carried down at the end of the day. Sarah's short sojourn in the canteen had proved useful for this knowledge.

If only she had been able to ask Mrs Pullman if the delivery was made at the same time each week, she thought wistfully, then shrugged. If she failed next week, then she would try the week after, she told herself firmly, flatly refusing to acknowledge the little ditty that crept into her mind at this point that went something like, 'sometime, never.'

CHAPTER FOUR

SARAH hung her one and only decent suit on the makeshift hangers, and sadly surveyed its creases, that she hoped would come out with hanging. It would be worn again when she made her bid for freedom, and although appearance was of small matter now, she did have some pride in her dress.

As she moved away, her foot touched something soft on the floor and looking down she saw that it was one of Martha's T-shirts, that had apparently got overlooked in the rush of leaving.

It was not an expensive item, and Sarah doubted whether Martha would recall its existence, it was certainly not worth the mailing fee should she make an effort to retrieve it.

All grist to the mill, Sarah thought, as she picked it up and held it away from her for inspection. It was certainly better than one of Mrs Pullman's dresses. All she had to do was to wash it, it would dry quickly in this torrid heat.

That was before she discovered that she was looking at the back of the shirt. When she turned it round and saw the deep vee in the front, she blinked and dropped the shirt as if it had burnt her fingers. Whatever else she wore, it wouldn't be that! Mrs Pullman's dresses would be more in keeping, she thought indignantly. She would have to be hard up if she came down to that, and if things got that bad, she would have to wear it back to front! Trust Martha to own a garment like that, although Sarah couldn't recall her wearing it. It was not the sort of thing one could miss noticing, not with Martha's cleavage!

The sight of the deep vee-fronted shirt brought back Sean Cartier's threats, threats that Sarah had simply refused to dwell on. He had only been trying to frighten her. She swallowed—and he had succeeded! She didn't want to think about what he had said, because in her book such situations simply didn't exist.

Sarah stuck her chin out. She had been hounded before by wolves, hadn't she? and she had learned to cope with them. Charles Ashley for one, and there were several others that she could mention. She ought to have got the hang of it by now, she told herself calmly.

Only she hadn't come across a man of Sean Cartier's standing before. As accomplished as Charles, no doubt, but with a ruthlessness that set him apart from the others.

A man who had no respect for her. She swallowed. She was entirely on her own. No dialling for reinforcements for her—police or fire brigade! She would have to get Sean Cartier's permission first, she thought wildly, recalling that flat voice on the other end of the line when she had tried to contact the outside world.

She took a deep breath. It was no use getting panicky. That would be playing the game his way, and it just wasn't on. If her luck held she would only have to put up with him for a week, so the thing to do was to play it coolly, she told herself sternly, although she didn't feel very cool at that point. Even let the wretched man think she had fallen for him. Sarah took a deep breath. In spite of his vanity, he hadn't been born yesterday, either. He would spot what she was up to in a flash, and most probably capitalise on it, and she would really be in a mess then.

Her eyes narrowed. He would play the cat-and-mouse game with her. He had said that she wouldn't know from one day to the other how he really felt about her, hadn't he? That could only mean that he intended to use his manly charms on her, by subtle flattery no doubt. Not that Sarah minded that, she could cope with that. It was what else he might have in mind that was really worrying her.

Her mind went back to the earlier dinners she had with him, before Charles Ashley had put a spoke in the wheel of their blossoming friendship. Sean had not put a foot wrong, and Sarah had appreciated this. There was no doubt that he had made a beeline towards her on the first day of their arrival. She could remember the way his blue eyes would automatically seek her out from the gaggle of press when they assembled for the daily bulletin, and it had come as no surprise when he had approached her later to have dinner with him.

Sarah was not a vain person, but life had taught her to expect such happenings. Her looks had gained her much unwelcome attention in the past, and they were her undoing now. If she had been plain, none of this would have happened. She would have got shot off the site in double quick time, but then there would have been no

need for any such action. If she had been plain,
Charles Ashley wouldn't have hankered after her,
or bothered to put her in this mess—not content
to just mention the past, but to tar her with the
same reputation as his own.

Sarah sighed. In a way she could understand
Sean Cartier's outraged feelings. He had, in his
eyes, made a fool of himself in the company of
several members of the press, and was still of the
opinion that Sarah's past was common knowledge
to all of them. Sarah drew a deep breath. Well, it
hadn't been, not until now, that was, and she
could imagine the interpretation Martha would
put on her continued absence from the scene. She
would easily accept the story of Sarah's engagement to Sean; with one of her knowledgeable
nods, clever Sarah had worked the oracle again.

Clever Sarah wasn't clever at all, Sarah
thought dispiritedly. She was in a mess, and she
couldn't see how she could get out of it. Her one
and only chance was in escape, and she was going
to need a lot of luck to accomplish that.

By way of distraction she picked up the file
that Sean had thrust at her, and began to study
its contents.

The trouble was that she couldn't concentrate
properly. She was dreading the dinner that she
was being forced to have with Sean. If she didn't
go to his quarters, then he would carry out his
threat of having it served in her room, and that
could lead to trouble, and she had had enough of
that for the time being.

What a fool she had been in telling him of her
plans to sue him! That was something she ought

to have kept up her sleeve. Now that he knew, it gave him an extra hold over her. He wasn't likely to let her go on her way once he had got tired of the game. He hadn't needed much excuse as it was, but she had handed him a far stronger one.

This time she was able to concentrate on the contents of the file. Anything rather than pursue her earlier train of thought, that was doing nothing for her pulse rate.

After studying the sheets of data for some time, Sarah thought she had the hang of it. It was just a question of copying the figures, once you recognised the scientific terms.

Sean's writing was bold and clear, much like the man he was, no half measures for him, she mused, and actually jumped when his voice came over the intercom. 'Dinner in thirty minutes,' he announced perfunctorily, and switched off.

Sarah glanced at her jeans and blouse. They were still presentable, and he wouldn't be expecting her to dress for dinner, she thought ironically, in an attempt to introduce some humour into the situation that went badly awry, for her pulse rate had gone up at the sound of his voice.

She spent as long as she could in the shower, and dawdled over brushing her hair, until she could no longer put off the moment she had been dreading, to go and join Sean for dinner.

A short walk across the main block brought her to Sean's quarters, and to take her mind off what was bound to be a miserable evening she recalled her first sight of the area, when they had arrived in various modes of transport, she and Martha sharing a cab with Charles Ashley, paying an extortionate amount for the trip. She recalled the surprise shown by all of them at the size of the site. No makeshift buildings here, but sturdy serviceable dwellings, and Charles had made some remark about it looking as if his source of information had not let him down. This site was built for a long stay, and was the property of the Bureau of Mineral Resources that covered a multitude of various surveys. It had been Sean Cartier's presence at the site that had sparked off the newsmen's interest.

There was something else that Sarah recalled at this time too, that did nothing to ease her situation, and that was that these surveys could go on for years.

She was in no mood for pleasantries when she met Sean at the door leading to his private quarters, and followed him through to the room he had selected as his dining room.

Sarah, of course, had been there before, but under much different circumstances. Then, she had been a welcome guest, and now she was under detention for goodness knew how long.

It had been Sandy, Mrs Pullman's niece, who had served the food before, when Sarah had been present, and she only hoped it would be Sandy again, and not her aunt.

In the event, Sarah's hopes were fulfilled, and it was Sandy who appeared a short while after Sarah's arrival, with a tray of covered dishes, and she would have stayed to serve the meal had Sean not sent her away with a flourish of his hand, indicating they they could manage, and little

Sandy had scuttled away before he changed his mind, in a manner that would have made Sarah smile any other time. It was plain that Sandy was in awe of the big boss, and had evidently received orders from her aunt not to make a nuisance of herself.

Up until Sandy had left, not a word had been spoken, Sean had contented himself with the fact that Sarah was there at his bidding, and Sarah had hardly looked at him since entering the room, and now that she did so, she saw that he had changed into evening wear, white shirt and dark pants, and she was provoked into saying acidly, 'You must excuse my not changing. I'm afraid my wardrobe, as I believe I did mention, is a bit on the sparse side.'

This only served to add to his enjoyment of the situation. 'Shall I have a word with Mrs Pullman, or will you?' he asked blandly, as he took the covers off the piping hot food and proceeded to ladle it out on to plates.

It was roast chicken with all the trimmings, but however delicious it smelt and looked, Sarah couldn't see herself enjoying one morsel, and she decided to ignore his taunt. She had already told him what she thought of that idea.

'On second thoughts,' he said musingly, as he placed a plate in front of her, 'it would be a shame to cover those gorgeous curves of yours, wouldn't it? I'm off to Darwin in a few days' time. I might pick you up something while I'm there.'

He might just as well have added, 'if you're good,' Sarah thought, as she stared down at her food. If he had wanted to make her feel like a kept woman, then he had succeeded, and she was careful to keep her eyes on her plate so that he should not see the hate she could feel welling up inside her. No matter what, she wasn't going to let him get under her skin.

'Eat up,' he said harshly. 'We can't have you fading away, can we?' he added silkily.

Sarah pushed her plate away. She would choke if she attempted to swallow one morsel.

'Have it your way,' Sean said lightly. 'Sooner or later you'll eat. I'd rather sooner, of course. Going without food makes you lightheaded, did you know that?' he sneered.

Sarah said nothing. He was baiting her, and she refused to rise.

'I'd like to take you to Darwin with me,' he went on conversationally. 'They've got some good restaurants there, although I may say I can't fault Mrs Pullman's cooking. It's just that there's more choice. They've also got some good night spots, and pretty well cover all types of entertainment,' he sighed loudly. 'It's not on, though, I'm afraid. I can't trust you, can I?'

If the look Sarah sent him was anything to go by, he had his answer!

He went on smoothly, 'Apart from our little private confrontation, you are now a security risk.'

Sarah blinked at this. 'Security risk?' she got out indignantly. 'If that's your excuse, it's a poor one, and wouldn't stand up in any court of law, and you know it!'

As soon as the words were out, Sarah regretted

them. The flash of fury in Sean's eyes told her it had been a mistake to bring the law into it.

'Remember what I told you about the 'C' factor?' he asked thinly. 'It wasn't a tale I told you to keep your journalistic instincts on the boil. It really exists, and apart from you, and me, and the head of my department, no one else knows it's been found, and that's the way it's staying, for the time being, anyway. So I should forget about bringing in the law,' he added meaningly, 'if you know what's good for you.'

Sarah stared at him. 'You deliberately gave me that information, didn't you?' she accused him angrily, fighting down an overwhelming desire to fling herself at him and pummel her fists hard on that solid-looking chest of his, if only to relieve her feelings.

He shrugged, and pushed away his bare plate. His appetite, it appeared, was not a bit impaired, she noticed sourly. 'It's not often I make a mistake,' he said grandly, 'but I guess you riled me into breaking a cardinal rule.'

Sarah looked away from him, unable to bear the mocking light in his blue eyes. It had been no mistake. She knew it, and he knew it!

She forced herself to stay calm and took a deep breath. 'If I gave you my solemn promise that I wouldn't divulge a word of what I'd learnt——' she began, but was stopped in mid-sentence by Sean's slow shake of his head.

'No dice,' he said abruptly. 'I couldn't risk it.' His answer was flat and very definite.

Sarah's lovely eyes met his cold ones. 'Because of Don, that's why, isn't it?' she said quietly.

'Did it ever occur to you that it could have been an accident?' she went on, determined to put her point of view to him.

His cold eyes continued to stare back at her, and Sarah's heart plummeted to an all-time low. He didn't believe her because he didn't want to believe her. It was as simple as that.

'If his death was an accident, then so was his grandmother's,' he said harshly. 'She worshipped Don. She didn't live much over a month after his death. Okay, so he liked his drink, but the same could be said for many men. He fell for you like a ton of bricks. You used him, didn't you? Your small county rag depended on the advertising revenue, and he did you proud, didn't he?' At Sarah's shocked look, he nodded grimly. 'Oh, yes, I was able to pick up that much, although the trail was cold by the time I got on to the scene. You were headed for the big time, weren't you? You were offered a post on one of the city papers, and you took it, without a backward glance at the man who loved you.'

Sarah's head spun. She hadn't known that Don had a grandmother. He had never mentioned her, but then he hadn't told her that he was related to Sean Cartier, either. It was true that she had been offered a post on the *Daily* the day after Don's death, and she had taken it, seeing it as an escape from her unhappiness. He had the facts right, but in the wrong order. She could have made an attempt to put the record straight, but he was in no mood to listen to her. He was determined to punish her, not only for Don's death, but his grandmother's, too.

'If you've finished,' he said harshly. 'You can get back to your quarters. I think I've had enough of your company for one day.'

Sarah needed no second bidding; she was out of her chair, and on her way, almost before he had finished the sentence.

Back in the quietness of her room, she gradually calmed down. Her situation had been bad enough before, but now—— She closed her eyes and shook her head.

She had been living in cloud cuckoo land, it seemed, when she thought that all she had to do was to walk off the site at the first given opportunity. She had never considered the possibility of finding herself on the wrong side of the law.

All Sean Cartier had to do was to alert the authorities. He'd do it, too, Sarah knew for certain. He could say that he had caught her snooping and considered that she was a security risk. She drew in a deep breath. The worst of it was, that the whole affair would be put under wraps. It would be her word against his, and she wouldn't stand a chance of proving her innocence.

It was detention here, or elsewhere, she thought, until the news was released, and goodness knew when that would be. Under the circumstances, she supposed she was lucky that she had a choice, she thought bitterly, that was the way that Sean Cartier would see it.

He could have had her sent away, but that wasn't in the scheme of things. She was to be his diversion while the site operations were closed down. In a few weeks the workforce would take off, leaving only a skeleton maintenance crew on site. Whether Mrs Pullman stayed on, Sarah had no idea, but thought not. The same could be said of Sean Cartier. If there was only paperwork to do, surely there was nothing to stop him going back to headquarters. A man of his standing in his profession would not be expected to hang around once the drilling operations ceased, and would not begin again for at least four months.

At this thought, Sarah shuddered. She couldn't imagine four months' detention in Sean Cartier's company. She was beginning to see now what he'd meant when he said that she would beg him to marry her. Four months was a long time. You couldn't go on hating someone—at least, not all the time. Not when they were the only contact you had with the outside world day in and day out. Some relationship or reliance was bound to result, and as he held all the cards, it was plain to see who would be relying on whom!

The fact that he hated her so much gave Sarah some consolation. He was not likely to force his attentions on her. The way he had looked at her as he spoke about Don's grandmother's death, told of his feelings. She could have been a rattlesnake, and one didn't take a rattlesnake to bed, so she could at least be grateful for that.

In one sense, it gave her a hold over him. Should he attempt any physical contact with her, she now knew how to handle it. All she had to do was to mention Don's name or his grandmother. Sarah closed her eyes. She wished that there was some other way, but she had no choice. She was fighting for her survival, but even so, things would have to get pretty bad before she used such despicable tactics.

A tap on her door brought her out of her musings with a jerk. Her first thought was that it was Sean Cartier, and she could think of no reason why he had followed her to her room, other than what she had had in mind only a few seconds ago, and swallowed convulsively before going to the door. She automatically straightened her slim shoulders. She knew what to do, didn't she? she told herself stoutly, as she opened the door.

It came as somewhat of an anti-climax to find Sandy outside the door with a tray of coffee in her hands. 'Mr Cartier's compliments,' she said, in the tone of voice that would have gone well with a wink, and handing the tray to Sarah, was off before Sarah could thank her.

The aroma of coffee drifted up to Sarah's bemused senses, as she stared at the tray in her hands. Her quick almost headlong dash from Sean's company, had happened before the coffee arrived, but why on earth had he bothered to send hers over? Was he now feeling sorry for her? she wondered. Then she shook her head. She didn't believe that for one moment. It was a way of confusing her, she was sure. He had said that she would never know where she stood with him.

Sarah grimaced as she carried the tray over to the small table that had served as Martha's makeshift dressing table, now mercifully free of the lotions that had littered the top. There were many things that she did not know, but one thing that she did know, and that was how Sean Cartier really felt about her.

The coffee was as good as it smelt, and Sarah enjoyed it. While she sipped her second cup, her thoughts roamed on. There had been one item of news in the short, uncomfortable dinner with Sean, that had given her spirits a lift. He was going to Darwin. He hadn't said when, or for how long, but it would give Sarah a welcome breathing space.

Perhaps she could make her bid for freedom then? But as soon as the thought was there, so was Sean's harsh statement of her being a security risk. It had been different before, for she had only envisaged causing him a few bad moments, a blow to his pride. The fly had got away.

He must know that she would never risk falling foul of the law. She drew in a deep breath. Whether he knew it or not. It wouldn't make any difference. All he had to do was to put a call out, and she would find herself on the wanted list.

It wouldn't matter to him one scrap what happened to her. One way or the other she was going to pay for what had happened to Don.

As Sean Cartier couldn't risk taking her to Darwin, so Sarah couldn't risk a breakout. Things were bad enough as it was, but at least her troubles were confined here, and if she was lucky, she would be packed off back to civilisation as soon as the news of the find was released.

So far, she thought, not too much damage had been done. If she played things coolly, when it was over, she would ask for her job back. The 'engagement' had been broken, she would tell Eddie. A mistake on both sides. Her firm lips twisted ironically on this thought. No need to go into details, she told herself. Her freedom would make up for all else—that, and the chance to get back to work. She didn't even care that her fine plans to sue Sean Cartier had gone up in smoke. She didn't want his money, or anything to do with him.

She let out a long ragged breath. She just wanted out.

CHAPTER FIVE

As nothing had been said about her taking any other meal with Sean, Sarah expected to take breakfast either in the canteen or in Mrs Pullman's kitchen, where Mrs Pullman and Sandy took their meals in between their work.

When she had awoken that morning, she had found herself ravenously hungry, and was looking forward to a visit to the canteen. Having spent the evening in her small room, she was in need of company; the only company she didn't need was that of Sean Cartier's.

She was in the act of leaving her room when she met Sandy carrying a tray. 'There's no need to bring anything over for me, Sandy. I was just coming to the canteen,' Sarah said, hoping her annoyance did not show in her voice. It was nice of Mrs Pullman to have thought about her.

Sandy grinned. 'No trouble,' she said brightly. 'Mr Cartier thought you might like some privacy. You're doing some work for him, aren't you?' she said. 'Aunt moaned a bit about it, but what Mr Cartier says goes, but it's a good job and she daren't upset him,' Sandy added confidentially.

Sarah thought if she heard the name of Cartier again, she would scream. However, she managed to hold her feelings in check. It wasn't Sandy's fault, after all, and no good would come of it if Sarah refused to accept his dictates.

Sarah took the tray from Sandy, who followed her into the room and collected the previous evening's coffee tray.

'Do you stay on during the wet?' Sarah asked her, seeing a chance to gain a little information from somewhere.

Sandy shook her head. 'I don't,' she said. 'Usually Aunt has a few months off, but she's not sure what's happening this time. Most of the men will have gone at the start, and there'll only be a few on site.' She frowned. 'Aunt said for security reasons,' she put her hand to her mouth. 'Oh dear, I'm not supposed to talk about that sort of thing.' Then she smiled at Sarah. 'Still, it's all right to talk to you, isn't it? You're one of us.'

Sarah was only too grateful for the fact that Sean Cartier was not in hearing distance of this remark from Sandy, but it was nice to know that someone trusted her.

Mrs Pullman might have moaned about having to supply an extra tray of food, one more, that was, from the boss's needs, but she had not stinted on Sarah's breakfast, and being hungry, Sarah did full justice to the meal.

As she had left, Sandy had said that she would be bringing Sarah's lunch around midday, and would collect the breakfast tray at the same time, so there was no need for Sarah to take the tray back when she had finished.

No excuse, either, for her to be wandering around the site, Sarah thought angrily. That was clever Mr Cartier's doing, too, no doubt!

At this point Sean's voice came over the intercom. 'I shall be over in fifteen minutes. I

trust you've finished your breakfast, and are
ready for work.'

Sarah made a face in the direction of the
loudspeaker, and gave a mock salute. 'All present
and correct, sir,' she said, as she finished the last
of her coffee, and re-stacked the tray with the
used plates.

Well before the fifteen minutes were up, Sarah
was in the next room where a typewriter had been
set up for her use, and the file Sean had given her
on the table next to it.

Home from home, she thought, as her eyes
rested on stacks of paper for typing, and
wondered if she was expected to use it all.

The sight of the typewriter brought back
memories she could have done without. In her
mind's eye she visualised the pandemonium that
would be going on in the *Daily*'s offices. At least,
it always looked like pandemonium, but in spite
of the feverish activity, everyone knew what they
were doing. They also knew that they were up
against a time limit.

It was as well for Sarah that Sean made his
autocratic entry at that point, because Sarah's
stiff upper lip was about to lose its rigidity, and
in another moment she would have given herself
the luxury of a few tears.

'You had a look at the file?' demanded Sean, as
he came into the room.

Sarah nodded but did not trust herself to say
anything.

'Good. It's quite straightforward. Just copy
what I've written down, and don't mix the sheets
up, because I didn't always number them. It

depended on how busy we were. Only use one sheet at a time for copying, then put it at the back of the file, and so on, with the rest. Got it?' he asked abruptly, and took the first sheet out of the file.

Sarah was forced to lean over him to look at the sheet, and a wave of masculine after-shave pervaded her senses, and she moved back slightly, but the move was duly noted by Sean, who looked at her with one eyebrow slightly raised in mockery. 'Can you see from there?' he asked silkily.

'Yes, thank you,' Sarah replied politely. 'One copy or two?' she asked, determined to show him that his tactics were not working, not visibly anyway.

'One,' Sean answered curtly. 'As long as you follow the order of the lines, the rest will be done at headquarters.'

In other words, this was just an exercise to give her something to do, she thought angrily, but wisely kept her thoughts to herself.

'I'll look in on you now and again,' Sean said breezily, before he left her to it.

A fat chance she would have of breaking out, should she still have it in mind, she told herself crossly, as she began to copy from the first sheet. All she had to look forward to now was his visit to Darwin, when, like it or not, she would take her meals in the canteen with Mrs Pullman, even if it was just to give her a change of scene.

As she worked, she tried not to think of the future, but it was hanging over her like a cloud in the background of her thoughts.

The summer monsoonal rains could last until April, and it was now early September. She didn't know a great deal about the Top End of the country, but she did know that. She knew, because she had once contemplated going on a tour of one of the National Parks in the area, where wild life abounded, and where it was only safe to travel with guides. Exploring on one's own was definitely discouraged, not only because of the vastness of the areas, but the inherent dangers within.

Her glance left the typewriter and she gazed out of the window on her left. Her look met the solid-looking block where the canteen was, and beyond that, more site buildings. She let out a deep sigh. It was hard to imagine that they could be anywhere near anything resembling a National Park, but she had seen that van, and Mrs Pullman had confirmed the fact that that was where the fruit had come from.

Distances, of course, meant nothing in this part of the country. The Park could be anything up to and over a hundred miles away, and probably was, she thought, as she recalled the arid, almost desert land the site had been built on.

There would be no deliveries during the wet, that much was certain, for Sarah recalled reading in one of the brochures about travel in the Top End during the wet, and how the Aboriginal people built their shelters on higher ground, and sleeping platforms were placed over slow wood fires to ward off insects.

That, and the fact that the site was built on land that ran parallel to Arnhem Land, the

Aboriginal reserve, would be bound to cut the site off during this period.

Sarah got back to work. She didn't have to go on cheering herself up with this kind of thinking, did she? There had to be a way out for her somewhere, although she had to admit that Sean Cartier couldn't have picked a better spot for her incarceration.

Slowly the day passed, and she got through a dozen of the sheets, interrupted intermittently by the arrival of Sean, who obviously took great pleasure at her absorption in her work.

One thing she was certain about was that she was not going over to have dinner with him that evening. She had stood enough from him to last her for quite some time, and come what may, she was staying in her quarters.

He must, however, have come to the conclusion that harassment did not improve the appetite, because shortly before she finished work that evening, he made a stiff-sounding apology to Sarah, that must have hurt his pride more than hers had been hurt the previous evening, leaving her no choice but to accept the olive branch, even though she knew it was a poor imitation of the real thing, like a plastic Christmas tree brought out year after year to suit the occasion.

From then on, she sensed a change in his tactics, and had been subjected to a barrage of charm that, to Sean's intense annoyance, hadn't worked either, for Sarah had remained unaffected, countering his various ploys with a coolness that matched his earlier comment of her hardheartedness.

During these evenings he would try to draw her out, using such subjects as her work, and appeared seemingly interested in her day-to-day routines, if a journalist could be said to have a routine, and in return for her answers, he supplied her with a few details of his own profession.

These were safe subjects to discuss, although Sarah was always ready for a blowback when her work was touched on. He had shown only too clearly what he thought of her, and the manner in which she procured her scoops, and she didn't believe for one minute that he had suddenly altered his opinion.

The plain fact of the matter was that he was lulling her into a false sense of security. Sarah knew it, but she was made of sterner stuff, and there were times when she could sense that he was keeping his feelings on a tight rein.

It was like living on the edge of a rumbling volcano, but she had to admire his strategy, and she always felt a great relief when she departed back to her quarters after they had had coffee.

It was a case of taking one day at a time, she thought, as she took a welcome cold shower, after being subjected to three evenings of undiluted charm from Sean.

The oppressive heat of the evening charged the whole atmosphere of the site. Like the lull before the storm, and waiting for the rains to come, so it was with her and Sean Cartier. It was too uneasy a truce to last.

By the time a week had passed, the thick file began to take on a slim look, although more sheets were constantly being added, as the work was still going on.

There was now only about a week to go before
the wet and the work force was packing. Even
Sarah could sense the feverish last-minute
preparations going on before the site was closed
down, and in spite of the torrid heat there was a
sense of relief in the air from the men about to go
on leave. She would catch snatches of songs sung
lustily by the workforce as their thoughts turned
towards the spell of leisure in store.

This reminded her of Sean's proposed visit to
Darwin. He had said nothing more about it, and
she could only hope that he hadn't changed his
mind. She didn't know how long he had been on
the site, but judging from the reams of notes on
strata levels, she thought at least six months.

It was small wonder that he got uptight, she
told herself, as she got ready to go over to dinner
with him. Six months' sojourn in this desert-like
outpost in the middle of nowhere would be
enough to strain anyone's good humour, although,
she mused, as she left her quarters, he ought by
now to be used to long stretches in these
conditions. His work would always be carried out
in remote regions, and for months at a time. It
could also, she thought, not quite so cheerfully,
make him a little odd.

He did not have an assistant, but she was sure
that this was from choice, and not from
parsimony from the Bureau. A man in his
position would only have to ask to receive, she
thought, as she crossed the square to the main
buildings, then she made a wry grimace. He had
got an assistant, hadn't he? Slave labour!

A loud wolf whistle rudely shattered her thoughts, and, startled, Sarah looked to her left, to find herself meeting the frankly admiring stares of a group of workmen clustered around two coaches standing in the compound.

This produced a chorus of whistles, and Sarah began to walk a little faster, embarrassment making her keep her eyes down as she neared her destination. They must have thought they were seeing a mirage, she thought dryly. She had been so successfully isolated from the workforce that apart from Mrs Pullman and Sandy, and of course the owner of that disembodied voice on the telephone, no one else knew of her existence.

As Sarah reached Sean's quarters, the wolf whistles stopped abruptly, as if a switch had been pulled, and glancing up, she saw the large figure of Sean standing by the open door with his arms across his powerful chest, and his hard gaze directed at the men, who went about their business with astonishing rapidity.

'Do you have to make an exhibition of yourself?' Sean growled, as he followed her into his quarters. 'I suppose you're missing all that adulation you used to get,' he added sneeringly.

Sarah took a deep breath. It was going to be one of those nights, and she doubted whether she would complete the first course of the dinner.

In a way she was relieved. He had been too polite for too long, and having to continually watch his words in the company of someone he detested was surely too much to ask of any man, and particularly this one, who had little time for niceties.

'I wasn't to know they were there, was I?' she replied, deliberately ignoring his taunts. 'They're going early, aren't they?' she asked, in an attempt to introduce a safer topic for conversation.

'We'd got as far as we could,' Sean answered grudgingly. 'There was no point in them hanging around.'

'Are they out of work now until the project starts again?' asked Sarah, determined to keep things on a level for as long as she could.

Sean gave her a contemptuous look. 'Of course not,' he said curtly. 'I thought you were bright,' he sneered. 'They'll have a couple of weeks off, then go to another site. They're mining engineers who know their job. They'll be back here when the dry sets in.'

Sarah gave up. He was determined to pick a fight with her, but she wasn't having any of it, and debated whether to go now, or wait until she received a few more insults. She longed to ask him when he was going to Darwin, but a sense of self-preservation warned her that this was not the time to chance her luck.

It was probably the thought of those men going off to enjoy themselves after a long stint on the job that had caused his bad temper. If it wasn't for her, he would be off, too, and it just went to show how stupid the whole thing was, she thought angrily, and found it hard to give Sandy a welcoming smile when she brought their tray over.

The meal was eaten in silence. Sean appeared to be lost in a reverie of his own, leaving Sarah to try and enjoy her meal.

It was lamb casserole, and Sarah, recalling Sean's comments about the restaurants in Darwin that gave you a choice of fare, could now sympathise with his feelings. It seemed only a day or so ago since they had last had lamb casserole.

If it wasn't casserole, it was stew, she thought, and the sweet would be jam sponge. Sarah could recite the week's menu by memory. The only changes were the days on which the meals were served, so that one never knew exactly what they were having, only that it would be one of the good old standbys.

Her thoughts roamed on as she took the lid off the expected jam sponge plate, and felt a mad urge to wave the lid in the air with a 'Hey presto! What do you think we've got for sweet?' comment, but glancing at the still absorbed Sean, she sighed inwardly as she took a small portion for herself, and thought longingly of the kind of meal she would order once this nightmare was over. She would love a salad, she thought wistfully, and something exotic to follow, like Peach Melba.

'We'll have some music after dinner,' Sean announced abruptly, breaking into Sarah's culinary excursions. 'You can dance, I suppose?' he demanded.

She stared at him, wondering if she had misheard him. 'I'm not very good,' she got out slowly, not liking this turn of events at all. What on earth had got into him?

'Didn't have much time for ordinary pursuits, I suppose,' he jeered. 'Not unless there was a story in it.'

Sarah could not argue this point, since it was true. She had been too busy in her chosen career to socialise, especially after Don's death. She had learnt a lesson that had held her in good stead for many years. Never again would she get involved with a man. If she was going to get worked up over anything, then it would be her job. You could keep romance; it only made a fool of you.

Sarah began to wish that she had lingered longer over her meal, or at least attempted to finish her portion of the casserole before pushing the plate aside half eaten, and going on to the sweet. It might have given her a bit more time to get used to the idea of dancing with Sean Cartier.

The bare fact that she had told the truth when she had said to him that she was not very good was not much consolation. He would get mad at her, she thought miserably, and goodness knew where that would lead.

When Sandy brought the coffee tray over, Sarah felt that time was running out on her, and Sandy's shy, 'I'm off now, Mr Cartier,' made her feel even more abandoned, as she listened to Sean's sincere-sounding reply that he hoped she enjoyed her leave, and he thanked her for looking after them, which produced a rosy blush from the highly gratified Sandy before she left them.

Sarah lingered over her coffee as long as she could, but she could sense Sean's impatience to get the ritual over with, and when she had finished she glumly followed him into the next room, that served as a lounge, although the furniture was spartan, necessities only, no fancy touches.

There was a tape recorder on a table next to the one and only easy chair, and Sean made for this as soon as they entered the room, and searching through a small pile of tapes beside the recorder, he selected three, one of which he put in the machine.

'You ought to be able to manage something simple like this,' he commented, as the strains of a haunting waltz filled the room.

'I wouldn't bet on it,' said Sarah. 'Couldn't we just listen to the music?' she asked. 'It's not really the weather for dancing, is it? You might be used to the heat, but I'm not,' she added for good measure.

'Scared?' Sean said softly.

'Of course not!' she replied angrily. 'Why should I be? I can't dance, and that's all there is to it,' she added crossly, as she sat down on the easy chair. 'It's not my fault you're not going on leave. It was your idea to keep me here. You could have gone to some night club this evening and had as many dances as you wanted,' she tacked on unwisely, too incensed to see the danger signals in his eyes.

'It's not too bad here, is it?' he asked silkily. 'Better than the treatment you would have received if I'd turned you in to the authorities.'

'And we both know why you didn't, don't we?' Sarah said bitterly. 'For the same reason you made me a security risk. Just to satisfy a personal grudge!'

'And to have a little company. You've forgotten that, haven't you?' he reminded her hatefully. 'As you rightly put it, I'm now on leave, and wish to enjoy myself. Right now I want to dance with you.' He suited the action to the words and pulled her out of the chair, and placing one arm around her slim waist and grasping her hand in his, said, 'It's easy when you know how. I'll teach you.'

Sarah was torn between laughter and tears, as she found herself being told to listen to the beat of the music, and was made to follow his steps across a floor space that was totally inadequate for dancing, and just when she thought she'd got the hang of it, she would miss a step and cannon into him.

'You're being deliberately dense!' he snapped angrily, the second time it happened. 'Wherever your brains are, they certainly don't reach your feet. It's so damn simple a child could do it!' he fumed at her.

Stung by this totally uncalled for remark, Sarah wrenched herself away from him. 'I told you I couldn't dance,' she said angrily. 'Perhaps you'll believe me now. As for being dense, what else do you expect? I'm cooped up here, typing those rotten figures all day. Seeing no one, apart from Sandy,' her breath came in gulps, as she struggled for composure, 'and if she hadn't found me some paperbacks to read in the evenings, I think I would have started talking to myself.' She swallowed. She wasn't going to break down now in front of him. She must have given him a lot of satisfaction already, seeing her in this state. 'F-find yourself another partner!' she got out, before she headed for the door.

She didn't make it, for Sean was there before

her, and grasping her arm in a hold that made her wince, he said softly, 'Why should I? I've already got one. The trouble with you is that you like your own way. Well, so do I. We dance, and this time you really try. I know you're missing the high life—well, exercise is good for tension. Let yourself go,' he commanded.

Sarah was past arguing with him. She was past a lot of things, particularly attempting to dance, and she stood stock still.

Sean yanked her into position, but she flung his hand away when he attempted to hold hers. The next minute she was in his arms, and he was kissing her with a ferocity that frightened her.

As abruptly as he had taken her in his arms, he released her, almost throwing her away from him. 'Now see what you've done!' he shouted at her, drawing his hand across his mouth in a gesture that suggested he was contaminated by her. 'Get the hell out of here before I lose all sense of proportion! It was what you were leading up to, wasn't it? I guess you're missing more than just company. Well, it so happens that I'm fussy. Now get!'

Sarah's head was high as she left. She had never hated anyone as much as she hated Sean Cartier at that moment.

If anyone had been working up to anything, he had. It was the sole reason he had insisted on dancing with her.

When she got back to her room, she leaned back against the closed door and let the tears spill over. His hateful remark about her missing more than company also applied to him rather than her. By all accounts he was no monk, and as he considered himself on leave, he'd probably got it all worked out. A few dreamy dances, and more than likely a few drinks in store as well.

She sighed raggedly. It hadn't worked. It was small wonder that he took it out on her, and would continue to do so, she thought miserably.

It couldn't go on, she told herself. Not now. She couldn't trust him. His instincts were male and predatory. He wouldn't give up. She had sensed the hunter in him, and he was out for the kill.

Sarah felt utterly weary. She didn't stand a chance. Sooner or later—— With mechanical actions, she carried out the evening chores she had had to adopt since her enforced stay at the site, and washed out her undies and cotton top. The only good thing that could be said about the heat was that the clothes dried quickly. Later, it would be considerably cooler, for the temperatures were those of the sub-tropics.

When she had finished, she was ready for bed. How long was it to go on? she wondered, as she lay wide-eyed in her bed, her body weary, but her brain still active.

She wasn't even sure what day it was, but she was vaguely aware that it was near the end of the month. All the days had rolled into one since the rush had started to get as up to date as possible before the site closed down. There were no such things as weekend breaks. There hadn't been for Sean Cartier, and so the same went for her.

Sarah didn't know what she would have done with a break anyway. At least she had something

to do during the daytime, and had even got used
to Sean stamping in at odd times of the day, as if
she could somehow vanish out of sight.

Not for the want of trying, she thought
unhappily. It was just that the cards were stacked
against her. There had been a slim chance, she
thought, as she recalled the Park van, but Sean
Cartier's threats had discouraged any attempt at
escape, as he had known it would.

She turned restlessly. He was right when he
had said things hadn't been too bad for her.
Apart from the fact that she had lost her freedom,
for the time being anyway, until news of the find
was allowed out, she hadn't had a lot to complain
about, only the loneliness.

She was still in one piece, but only just, and
the thought of having to go over to his quarters
the next evening was unendurable.

As far as she was concerned the volcano had
erupted, and she would have to spend each
evening dodging the sparks from the inferno.

Anything would be better than that, she
thought. He hated her enough now, but if
anything should happen, he would hate himself
as well. She shivered. No matter what, she wasn't
going to let that happen. It would be worth the
risk of being picked up by the authorities; at least
she would be out of his vicinity.

She sat up suddenly. The coaches, she thought.
She had seen two in the square that day. Would
there be more? and if so, what were the chances
of her stowing herself aboard?

Recalling the wolf whistles, Sarah shook her
head. She couldn't ask for a lift without saying

why she had to get out. There was so much security there that each man's pass would be checked.

Her mind went back to the Park van. Would he still be delivering the fruit? There was a small chance that he would, for the decision to close down appeared to have been a quick one, going perhaps on the weather forecast.

Sarah scrambled out of bed and finding her shoulder bag hunted in it for her diary. Then she counted the days from the day she had known the date, when she had typed a letter for Sean. It was Thursday tomorrow! She recounted to make sure, but it came out the same.

Come hell or high water, she was going to be hanging around the canteen from early afternoon onwards. If the Park van did come, she intended to leave in it.

Surely this time her luck would change, and things would go right for her. It wasn't as if she was guilty of the crime she was being made to pay for. If there was any justice in the world, she would get away.

The first thing Sarah did the next morning was to pack her silk suit and all her belongings into her overnight case, ready to be picked up at a moment's notice, and stuff it under the bed, remembering that Sandy would bring her breakfast over later; then recalled that Sandy had gone yesterday.

In that case, Sarah told herself, she would go over to the canteen to save Mrs Pullman lugging her breakfast over. It would serve as a good excuse for her to find out if the Park van was expected to call, and if so, at what time. It would be easier for Sarah if she knew precisely what time it would be there, but she had to be careful not to arouse Mrs Pullman's suspicions.

She went over to the canteen early. It was strange to hear no other sounds of human industry. Like a ghost town, she thought, as she entered the canteen kitchen to find Mrs Pullman just sitting down to her breakfast.

At the sight of Sarah, she frowned. 'Thought you'd have gone with Mr Cartier,' she said.

Sarah blinked, but her heart leapt joyfully. 'Has he gone?' she asked.

Mrs Pullman gave her an old-fashioned look, that told Sarah that she had been perfectly right when she had suspected that Mrs Pullman was of the opinion that Sarah was chasing Sean Cartier, who it appeared had got away from her clutches. Her look said that she had seen it all before, and that no self-respecting young lady ought to throw herself at a man like that. In her opinion, Sarah had got her come-uppance; men didn't respect girls like that.

Sarah tried to look abashed, but it was difficult, for she felt as if a great weight had been taken off her shoulders. 'Where's he gone, do you know?' she asked Mrs Pullman, who had got up to get her breakfast, but Sarah motioned her to sit down again. 'Finish your breakfast. I can get mine. I only want toast,' she insisted.

Slightly mollified, Mrs Pullman did as she was bid, and poured her out a cup of tea. 'Darwin,' she said. 'Left on the last coach, early this morning. Didn't say anything about you still being here. I'm due off myself around four,' she said, savouring the thought of time off, then she suddenly recollected Sarah's presence. 'There's plenty of stuff in the freezer, for a week or two at least. I hadn't banked on the site closing down so early, there must have been a bad forecast,' she said musingly.

'What about the maintenance staff?' asked Sarah, wondering if that was another job that Sean had in mind for her, cooking for them!

'Oh, they have a kitchen of sorts down in the social club. Mostly tinned stuff. It's not worth keeping the canteen open for them—besides,' Mrs Pullman added darkly, 'I don't want them mucking up my kitchen.'

'So there won't be a delivery of fresh fruit today?' Sarah asked idly, although she held her breath for the answer.

Mrs Pullman nodded. 'Didn't have time to cancel it,' she said. 'Still, it won't go amiss. They'll be glad enough of it down at the social club.'

Sarah let out her breath, and wondered if she dared risk carrying out a plan that had suddenly presented itself to her. If she was right about Mrs Pullman's thoughts about her, then it would work; if she wasn't, then she would be no better off than she was before.

She carefully buttered her toast, and said thoughtfully, as if speaking to herself, 'I guess it's time to move on.' She looked at Mrs Pullman. 'You can't win them all, can you?' she said, and sighed. 'He could have told me he was going to Darwin,' she added, in what she hoped sounded a pettish tone. 'So that's that. Do you think there's any chance of the Park van driver giving me a lift? No one seems to have any transport here, and as there's no more coaches leaving, I'll have to make my own arrangements.'

Mrs Pullman's look said it all. She didn't think there was much point in Sarah hanging around either, not now that she had been given the big brush-off. 'He might,' she said consideringly. 'I can't offer you a lift. My son's collecting me, and we don't go anywhere near the main routes. We'll see what he says.'

Sarah could almost smell freedom. There was no reason why the driver should refuse to give her a lift to the Park; he'd probably be glad of the company, she thought, and she could surely find other transport there to take her back to civilisation!

CHAPTER SIX

IN gratitude for Mrs Pullman's co-operation in assisting her escape, although that good lady would have been most put out had she known the reason for Sarah's over-long stay at the site, Sarah asked if there was anything she could do to help her in closing down the canteen, now that she was without Sandy's help, and her offer was accepted.

As they washed down tables and shelves, Sarah made general conversation with the manageress. She wondered why Sandy had gone the day before her aunt, and whether the decision to let Mrs Pullman go had been a sudden one, for she recalled Sandy saying that her aunt sometimes stayed on at the site.

It turned out that Sandy's boy-friend was an apprentice there, and she had gone back with him to meet his family. 'I don't know what my sister will have to say about that,' mused Mrs Pullman. 'She considers Sandy's a mite too young to start courting, but she forgets how it was when we were seventeen. I was married at eighteen, and she was married at nineteen. Just as well, come to think of it,' she added, as she paused for a moment, then started polishing vigorously. 'Was widowed twenty years later, so was Cathy—they worked together. A storm uprooted a tree and landed it right across the road—pitch black it was.

They didn't stand a chance.' She sniffed.
'There's no sense in trying to hang on to the
young ones. They do what they want to do these
days,' she went on, hastily changing the subject,
as if she could sense Sarah's sympathy. 'It's all
different these days,' she added darkly.

Sarah was certain that Mrs Pullman's thoughts
were not entirely on Sandy when she made that
pronouncement, and she hastily introduced
another subject. Had it been a sudden decision
for her to take leave?

The answer was as Sarah had thought. It had
been sudden. Mrs Pullman would normally have
stayed on if the big boss was still around, and it
was plain that she considered that Sean Cartier
had left the site for quite some time.

Sarah wasn't really convinced about this, for
she felt that it would be just like him to expect
her to do the cooking as well as the typing. She
had complained about the figure work and the
loneliness, and he would consider that more work
would soon cure that.

Shortly after lunch they went their separate
ways. Mrs Pullman to pack her case, and no
doubt take a short nap afterwards, and Sarah to
generally tidy up. Her things were already
packed.

Mrs Pullman told her that the Park van could
be expected any time after three, and Sara replied
that she would be back at the canteen well before
that, in case he was early.

When she had finished putting everything to
rights in her room, she went into the small room
she had used as an office, and noticed that the file

had gone, and for the first time she began to believe that Mrs Pullman had been right in assuming that Sean Cartier did not intend to return for quite some time.

As Sarah stared around her, she saw that there was not a trace of any work in the room. Even the waste paper basket had been emptied.

She drew in a long breath. Sean Cartier's decision to go to Darwin had been an overnight one. It was because of what had happened. He couldn't trust himself not to repeat his advances.

Perhaps he hoped she would escape? Her forehead creased in thought. It would be the perfect answer for him. He would know that her only wish would be to keep out of his vicinity. He didn't really believe she was a security risk, even though he had accused her of not being very bright; she would have to be an absolute dullard if she was stupid enough to publish news of the find.

No, she mused, it was just an excuse to pay her out. Why, if she had been a real security threat, he would have warned Mrs Pullman to keep an eye on her, and he hadn't!

Sarah took a deep breath. As far as he was concerned, the game was over. She closed her eyes as a feeling of deep relief spread over her. It was over! All she had to do was to get to the National Park and beg a lift from one of the coaches or from private transport. She would prefer not to go back to Darwin, but she knew she had no choice in the matter.

In any case, it would be dark by the time they got to Darwin, and surely that was all to the good? Not that there was a chance that she would run into Sean Cartier, he would be too busy whooping it up in some night spot to even give her a thought.

She would book in at a small hotel, and with luck, be on the first plane out and on her way home before His Lordship was awake.

In her mind's eye she saw herself striding up the steps of the *Daily* entrance and walking through reception, giving an idle wave to Marge at her desk, and going on through to the maze of small offices with the typewriters blazing away. She smiled, it was doubtful whether they would notice her as she made her way to the editor's office.

From then on, it would be easy. She would not go into details, her thoughts remained the same on this. The less said the better. The 'engagement' was off! This produced another smile from Sarah, and after a glance at her watch, she went back to her room and gathered up her case, then made her way to the canteen to await the Park van.

As it happened the van was early, and arrived at a quarter to three. Mrs Pullman was still in her quarters, and Sarah, anxious to be on her way, approached the driver when he got out of his van to make the delivery.

Flashing her press card at him, and giving him a smile that made him blink, Sarah asked if he'd mind giving her a lift out of the site. She had come to see Mr Cartier, she explained, and found he was on leave. Now she was stuck without transport, and could he oblige?

It was as well for Sarah that the van driver was not all that bright, for had this actually been the case, she would never have got past the gate in the first place.

As in the past, the showing of the press card did wonders. It was an open sesame to otherwise closed doors, and with a grin the driver said he would be glad to have her aboard. By the time Mrs Pullman had got to the canteen, the fruit had been delivered and the driver waiting for her signature.

There were a few bad moments for Sarah when Mrs Pullman mentioned the pass she would have to have before she got past the gates, and in dismay she could see all her hopes going up in smoke, until Mrs Pullman reminded her of the small blue plastic badge they had all been given to wear on their lapels while on the site, and after a feverish search in her shoulder bag, Sarah found hers tucked away at the bottom of her bag. Since becoming, or being forced to become a member of staff, she had not had to display the badge. That rule was confined to visitors only.

She managed to contain her feelings of utter relief as she produced the badge when they were stopped at the gate on the way out, and then waved out of the site, and she blessed Mrs Pullman for her foresight in reminding her about the badge. In her heightened state of apprehension, she might well have burst into tears when challenged for her pass, and found herself being held in custody while a few more enquiries were made, and that meant contacting the big boss— and that meant——

Sarah felt like bursting into song as they left the site behind them. She had made it! She hadn't been able to bring herself to really believe that she could do it, until now, and if Eddie had any more stories that concerned or even vaguely concerned the Bureau of Mineral Researches, he would have to consign them to someone else. Wild horses wouldn't drag her back to Sean Cartier's dominion!

She found that she had been wrong in assuming that the National Park would be at least a hundred miles from the site, because it turned out to be only thirty miles away.

In return for replying to the driver's curious questions about the life of a journalist, Sarah extracted information about the Park.

Their destination, she learned, was to be Jim Jim, a popular visiting area, not only because of its spectacular falls and great beauty, but because it catered for the tourist in providing motel accommodation.

Already the scenery was changing, she noticed, as they sped on along the Arnhem Highway, the desert-like scenery being replaced by greenery. The change was so dramatic that she had to blink once or twice to convince herself that she was not dreaming. She could see and hear the screech of the brightly coloured parakeets as they flew from tree to tree, in what was surely paradise after the aridity that reigned only twenty miles distant.

Seeing deep gorges ahead of them, Sarah was reminded of the brochure she had studied, and she asked the driver if they might spot a crocodile.

This produced a grin from the driver. 'Going to do a feature on the Park?' he asked, then said, 'We might, but you'd really have to go deeper into the reserve. There's plenty of guides who can show you. You'd have to book up, of course. They're pretty busy right now, there's a last-minute rush before the wet.' His eyes scanned the horizon. 'Signs are it's not too far ahead,' he added.

Sarah had no wish to get trapped in that part of the world, and as much as she would have liked to have booked herself up for a tour, she daren't risk it. It was a bit too near a certain person's territory. All he would have to do was to go and collect her if he felt so inclined, but opportunity would be a fine thing, she told herself, and she wasn't about to allow that to happen.

As soon as they arrived at Jim Jim, after profusely thanking the driver, Sarah went to the motel and enquired about transport back to Darwin. After being asked if she had missed her coach, she had to admit that she had got private transport to the Park, but now needed to get back to Darwin under her own steam.

The receptionist was plainly of the opinion that she had come with a boy-friend, had a row, and preferred to go it alone. Sarah didn't care what she thought, as long as she could provide some sort of transport for her.

'Well, there's coach number seven,' the receptionist said. 'The driver will be in the café. He's due to leave in ten minutes. He didn't come in with a full quota, so he'll probably take you.'

Sarah could have hugged the receptionist, who

in a way reminded her of Mrs Pullman, a little younger, but of the same opinion as the canteen manageress. Her expression had said it all—trips of that nature should never be undertaken with someone you didn't know very well. It was just asking for trouble.

The café was really a part of the motel, only one had to go outside and enter by another door, and as there were only a few people in the café, it was not hard for Sarah to spot the coach driver, since he was the only one there that sported a cap with the legend 'Sunset Tours' across the front.

The name of the firm rang a bell, of course, for Sarah recalled that that had been the name of the coach that had got stuck in a rut not far from the site, and she devoutly hoped that history would not repeat itself on the way back to Darwin.

She had no trouble in securing herself a seat on the coach, and she just had time for a cup of tea before she followed the driver's tall back out of the café and to the coach lined up with others at the back of the motel.

As she settled down in the back of the coach, Sarah looked at her watch. The coach was leaving at four forty-five, and the estimated time of arrival in Darwin would be around ten o'clock. She would then have to book in for the night, and be off, with luck, on the first flight out to Sydney the next morning.

After so much activity, she was physically and mentally tired, and not long after the coach had left Jim Jim she was sound asleep.

The next thing she knew was a buzz of activity around her, that somehow got through the fog of sleep, and the coach driver calling out 'Darwin' for the benefit of others like Sarah, who passed the journey in sleep.

The bright lights of the terminus made her blink as she gathered her overnight case from the rack above her and sleepily followed the other passengers out of the coach.

Her feet were on the last step of the coach when she found herself caught in an embrace that knocked the wind out of her sails. 'Darling! So glad you could make it,' said a voice that Sarah had hoped never to hear again, and for a minute or so she thought she must still be dreaming, but when the voice said close to her right ear, 'You didn't think it was going to be that easy, did you?' she came down to earth with a bump.

With his hard arm around her waist, pinioning her to his side, Sean bundled her to the car park, and before she could utter a word, for she was still in shock, he had pushed her into a Land Rover, where she sat for a moment trying to get her breath back. A second later he was in the driving seat and starting the engine.

All Sarah could think of was that they were heading back to the site, back to the wilds, with no Mrs Pullman, and no one else near her but this hateful man sitting beside her.

She was beyond tears, she knew when she was beaten. What a fool she had been in thinking he would let her go as easily as that! He had had it all worked out, she thought dully.

His next words more or less confirmed this. 'I checked with the gate,' he said casually, 'I thought you might get smart. Still, it gave you a day out, I suppose,' he added in an amused voice, then gave her a hard look. 'Didn't communicate with anyone, did you?' he asked harshly, then answered his own question. 'No, you wouldn't be that much of a fool, would you? You just wanted to get back to the bright lights, didn't you? I'm afraid that's still out for you. We're going to my place. There's no bus routes there, and no bright lights either.'

Sarah said nothing. She didn't think there could be any worse place than the site, but what he had just said showed her that there could be. Goodness only knew where they were heading now. To some shack in the wilderness, she presumed, and almost shuddered. At least she had had some privacy before. Sean must have had this place in mind all along, she thought bitterly, as she recalled his words that she would be begging him to marry her. It didn't leave much to the imagination.

'We'll make one stop,' he said curtly, breaking into her miserable musings, as he leant forward towards her side, an action that made her cringe away from him, but he seemed not to notice it as he felt for a catch on the dashboard in front of her, and finding it, brought a small flap down. 'There's a flask of coffee in there,' he said, 'help yourself when you want it. There's some sandwiches, too. We're only stopping for gas,' he added perfunctorily.

Sarah was neither hungry nor thirsty. She wanted nothing from this man, and with an angry gesture she pushed the flap back into position.

'Suit yourself,' he said airily, then concentrated on his driving.

For a while Sarah watched the road too, but as it seemed an endless red dirt track that seemed to lead further and further into the wilderness, she soon found herself being lulled into sleep. For a time she fought against it, fearful that she would eventually lean against the driver, then as the urge to close her eyes became too strong to resist, she compromised by turning her head towards the window on her side. If she couldn't stay awake then at least she could ensure that she stayed well away from the man who had become the bane of her life.

It seemed no time at all before she was being roughly awoken, and her sleep-clogged senses became aware that they had stopped.

They were in the courtyard of a petrol station, and Sean was climbing out of the Land Rover. 'There's a powder room at the back,' he said harshly. 'Step on it. I want to be off as soon as we've filled up.'

For a moment Sarah was tempted to stay put, but then sense got through. She didn't know how long they would have to travel before they eventually arrived, and as her mind became more active, it occurred to her that there might be a chance to use a telephone.

At this stage of the game, she needed help badly, and she wasn't fussy who gave it to her. If only she could get through to the *Daily*, she thought, as she climbed out and went in search of the powder room.

The brightly lit area made her blink until she had adjusted her vision, and looking at her watch she saw that it was twelve-thirty. There was always someone on duty in the news room, if only she could get to make the call.

As she left the powder room, she was half surprised to find that Sean was not waiting right outside for her, just in case she made a break for it, but from what she could see from the dim lighted courtyard of the garage, it was in the middle of nowhere, and beyond it were pools of inky darkness.

'Cattle country,' said Sean, looming up beside her out of the gloom. 'Hundreds of kilometres of it,' he added meaningly. 'Ready?'

It was not a question but an order, and Sarah looked past him to the wizened old man who stood by the door of the paying in area, and who lifted a hand in salute. 'Day Sean,' he wheezed, before he disappeared from sight.

Everything, thought Sarah unhappily, as she got back into the Land Rover, seemed to be conspiring against her. Even if she had got to that pay phone she had spotted behind the form of the old man before he had closed the door behind him, she wouldn't have been given the chance to make a call. Not if Sean Cartier gave the word. The man knew him, and he didn't know her, it was as simple as that.

On their way again, she saw a difference in the road. It was no longer a red dirt track, but now appeared to be a small highway, the sort of road that eventually led somewhere, although where, she had no idea.

She saw fences, too, that confirmed Sean Cartier's statement that this was cattle country, and she wondered if he owned a station. She knew that stations could be hundreds of miles apart. As soon as this thought came to her, she threw it out. What would he do with a station? His work took him all over the country.

He was more likely to know someone who did own a station, and perhaps rent some land from him. Sarah sighed inwardly. She was back to that shack again. His very work would make him a loner, she concluded.

By this time she was thirsty, and her thoughts went to the flask behind the flap in front of her. Even if she were to get it out, she couldn't see how she could drink the coffee, not at the speed they were doing, and the sudden lurches over rough patches in the road that they would go over now and again. She could ask him to pull up for a while, she thought, but she didn't want to ask this man anything, she told herself stubbornly.

As if sensing her thoughts, Sean said abruptly, 'We should be there in twenty minutes.'

Sarah stared ahead of her, then her eyes went to the sky ablaze with stars that were bigger and brighter than she had ever seen. That was something else she had read in the brochures, she thought wearily. If only she had kept to her original plan and hidden herself away in the van, it would have been days before he would have found her, even if he had bothered to look for her.

She recalled what he had said about her not being stupid enough to make contact with her paper and pass on what was apparently a state secret. He had been sure of that, and it underlined his real reason for denying her her liberty.

'I was coming back tomorrow,' Sean said, uncannily homing in on her thoughts. 'We'd have made this journey a little later. You could have saved yourself a trip to the Park. I'd have found you anyway—there was nowhere else you could have gone. As soon as I knew what time the van had left, the rest was easy. I didn't think you'd hang around seeing the sights, and I was right, wasn't I?' he added grimly.

'I only wish I had!' Sarah declared vehemently. 'At least I'd have had one evening in peace.' She stared at her hands. 'Mrs Pullman thought you'd gone on leave.'

She felt Sean glance at her. 'And you hoped she was right?' he said silkily.

'Not at first,' she admitted unwillingly. 'But when I saw that you'd cleared the desk and taken all the notes with you, then I did.'

'Couldn't take any chances, could I?' Sean replied airily, to Sarah's fury. 'I slipped up once with you. I'm not likely to do so again.'

She glanced towards his hard profile. He was not talking about classified information, she was certain. He had made a fool of himself over her, in the same way that he thought his cousin Don had.

All this was just an exercise to satisfy his bruised pride. He was still certain that she had known of his connection with Don, and had played him on the same line, confident of her success. According to his biased thinking, she had had plenty of experience at the game.

Suddenly the road, more of a track now, branched off, and Sean's strong hands swung the wheel over sharply as they took a bend.

All Sarah could see was a dim light in the
distance that got steadily brighter as they
approached. It was a porch light that partially lit
a covered verandah that ran the length of the
building.

It was a building, and not a shack as she had
imagined, and she only hoped that this would
turn out to be their destination, for although
most of the structure was in darkness, it gave the
impression of roomy accommodation. On the
other hand, it might be the homestead of the
owner of the property.

If this was the case, and it must be getting on
for two in the morning, it was hardly a suitable
time for a call, and Sarah was quite prepared for
them to sail right by.

In the event, Sean swept right up to the
homestead, and a partially relieved Sarah found
her belongings, that had been unceremoniously
dumped in the back of the Land Rover at the
start of their journey, now thrown back at her.

At this moment the homestead door opened
and light spilled out on to the front area, and
Sarah saw a profusion of flowering shrubs at the
base of the verandah.

She saw something else, too, that was there one
minute, and gone the next. An apparition in a
long white nightshirt that had appeared as soon
as they had drawn up in front of the house, and
disappeared with amazing rapidity as she got out
of the Land Rover. For a startled moment Sarah
wondered if she had seen a ghost.

A few minutes later, however, her fears were
dispelled by the appearance of a small stout

Chinese, now hastily dressed in checked shirt and dark trousers, smiling and nodding a welcome as he relieved her of her case.

'Lin, this is Miss Helm. She's staying a while with us. Put her in the back room. She'll be helping out with the chores,' Sean announced haughtily, and his look forbade any comment from the astounded Chinese, whose slant-eyed look went perplexedly from his boss to Sarah, then with a little polite bow, he murmured, 'Missy follow me,' and proceeded to lead the way to wherever her quarters would be.

Sarah was only too pleased to leave Sean Cartier's presence. She felt a burning resentment at the introduction. How dared he? He had made it quite plain from the start that she was a nobody and was being made to pay for her keep by helping out with the chores.

From the little Chinese's expression on learning which room Sarah had been allotted, she gathered it would be little more than an attic. Servants' quarters, no doubt, but she didn't mind that. She was only too relieved that she would not be living in close proximity with that detestable man.

After walking down a passage and turning right at the end, they eventually came to the room. She could almost feel the embarrassment of the small manservant as he indicated that they had arrived.

The room was much as Sarah had expected. Small, and sparse. The single divan had a worn-looking coverlet on the top. An ancient-looking home-made dressing table, and a rickety chair, that stood on worn lino, completed the furnishings. It was the sort of room given to casual labourers, working their way from station to station; even so, it was better than Sarah's lurid earlier imaginations of the quarters she would find herself sharing with Sean Cartier, and she was not complaining.

While she was taking in the room, Lin was opening the drawers of the dressing table and taking out sheets and a pillow case, with which he proceeded to make the bed.

'I'll do that,' Sarah said hastily, now beginning to feel embarrassed. 'I'm sorry you've been put to such trouble.'

'No trouble,' Lin replied in his sing-song voice, but he let Sarah carry on with making the bed. 'Missy come to the kitchen when ready. Lin make hot drink and maybe food if hungry,' and with a little swift bow, he left her.

After she had made the bed, Sarah searched for the bathroom, hoping that one had been provided for the servants' quarters, and that she wasn't expected to use a tap in the yard.

She felt travel-stained and incredibly tired, which was not surprising considering how far she had travelled that day, and gave a sigh of relief when two doors down from her room she found a small bathroom with shower.

As in her room, there were only the bare essentials, but there was a mirror that she was able to use to smarten up her appearance. She was determined not to let things get her down. It could have been much worse, she told herself, before going to find Lin and the promised hot drink.

CHAPTER SEVEN

AFTER the initial uncomfortable opening of her acquaintance with Lin, Sarah was soon put at ease by his gentle manner.

It was plain that he was somewhat confused by her presence, not to mention his boss's attitude towards her, but being the gentleman he was, he accepted the situation as it was presented to him.

Only once did his natural curiosity make him ask her a question, and that was on that first night while Sarah sat sipping delicious coffee, and tucking into equally delicious small sandwiches that he had prepared for her.

'You take something from boss?' he asked, his brown liquid eyes sympathetic, and not accusing.

Sarah, in the act of swallowing the last of the sandwiches, stared at him, her fine brows raised in amazement. 'Of course not!' she said indignantly, although, she mused, if there was such a thing as stealing one's pride—'No,' she repeated, half to herself, 'it's not as simple as that.'

Lin surveyed her silently for a moment, then nodded his head. 'You steal something,' he said enigmatically, and that was the end of the matter as far as he was concerned.

Thief or vagabond, it made no difference to Lin, Sarah discovered as time went by. He treated her with the same respect that he would have treated the woman of the house.

Little jobs were found for her, but they were only menial tasks, just something to keep her occupied, she noted. The only real assistance she was allowed to give him was in the preparation of meals. He was a first rate cook, and Sarah was fascinated by the stock of herbs and culinary aids in the larder, and had asked Lin to teach her the art of cooking.

She had nothing else to occupy her time. Sean Cartier had kept his distance. She did not see him for the first three days since he had brought her to Wallaby Ridge—the name, she had since learned, of the homestead, that was once a cattle station, and had now been taken over by a neighbouring station, the Cartier family holding on to the homestead.

All this Sarah had been told by Lin, who had worked for the family since he was seventeen, and that was many years ago, judging by the little man's wrinkled skin.

Although Sarah had not seen Sean, she knew he was there, his quarters being mercifully over the other side of the large homestead, and of course, by the preparation of the meals. She learned which were his favourite dishes, beautifully prepared and served by Lin, and she found time to wonder how he put up with the rough and ready fare served to him in his various excursions into the wilds.

Four days after she had arrived, the homestead had a visitor. Sarah, busy chopping up mint, had not heard the car draw up in front of the homestead, but Lin's sharp ears had, and as it was close to lunchtime, and visitors in that part of the

world were rare, all operations for lunch were
suspended on the likelihood of an extra place
being laid, or several extra places, depending on
the number of visitors.

A few minutes later, Sean entered the kitchen,
and Sarah, with her back to the door, and in the
act of washing her hands at the large chromium
plated sink unit, spun round at the sound of his
voice.

She might have been Scotch mist for all the attention he gave her; his orders were for Lin to prepare
another place in the dining room for his visitor.

Sean had totally ignored Sarah's presence, but
not so his visitor—a tall elegant woman, raven-
haired, and a beauty to boot, who frankly stared
at her with dark assessing eyes, and who stood
behind Sean, and now walked forward. 'How are
you, Lin?' she asked in a husky voice, although
her eyes never left Sarah, standing by the sink
with a small flimsy pinny round her small waist
that Lin had unearthed for her, and now
beginning to resent the marked attention she was
getting from the woman. 'Long time, no see,' the
woman went on, obliquely addressing Lin.

Lin's polite reply was hardly finished before
Sean ushered the woman out of the kitchen, in a
manner that told of his annoyance at the woman's
intrusion. He had clearly not invited her to follow
him.

Lin smiled, and nodded sagely. 'That missy
mad on boss,' he said in his sing-song voice. 'No
like other missy,' he added with a wicked grin.
'She'll be back,' he stated, in his inimitable way,
as he set to the task of providing an extra lunch.

'Does she usually come to the kitchen?' asked Sarah, wondering if there was a chance for news of her incarceration getting to the outside world, and therefore a chance for liberation.

Lin shook his head. 'Why she want see old Lin?' he asked simply, and Sarah's hopes began to rise. The woman had known that Sarah was there, that much was obvious, and in all probability was at that very moment trying to discover her identity.

Sarah's brows creased in thought. But if she knew that she was there, then surely she knew who she was! Then she had the answer. 'So that's it!' she said half to herself, but Lin heard her.

'So?' he said, waiting for her to enlighten him.

'It must have been the garage man,' said Sarah. 'We stopped just before we got here,' she added, by way of explanation, which wasn't very enlightening, but Lin understood, and nodded.

'Old Joe talk too much,' he commented. 'Boss not like that,' he shook his head. 'Old Joe up for high jump,' he added, and this time gave another of his knowing nods.

Lin's confident prediction that Pauline Cook, the woman who, according to Lin, was 'mad about the boss' would be back proved a non-starter, and Sarah could only assume that Sean, in his usual high-handed way, had made certain that she wouldn't.

Sarah had no idea what excuse he had given for her presence in his home, but whatever it was, she was sure that Miss Cook would not believe it, and would not let it rest at that.

Like Lin, Sarah was confident of another visit,

if not the next day, then the day after, and she
wondered if she could contrive to have a few
words with her. A jealous woman could be of
invaluable help, particularly in this instance, she
thought. Once her mind was set at rest against
the possibility that Sarah was after her man,
Sarah was sure that she would have an ally in
assisting her removal from the homestead in the
very near future.

In the event, by the time several days had gone
by, and no sign of Miss Cook had appeared on
the horizon, Sarah's hopes began to fade, more so
because Sean was absent from dinner on at least
three occasions, and was, according to Lin,
paying his respects to the Cook Station. Colin
Cook, Pauline's father, had taken over the station
from the Cartiers, and built himself a homestead
over the ridge some fifteen miles away.

Sean Cartier was making doubly sure of
keeping Pauline away from the homestead by
spending his time at the Cook station, Sarah
conceded bitterly, as she tucked into Lin's
delicious stuffed shoulder of lamb, with buttered
potatoes and tender green beans.

Most of her evenings were spent now in either
playing Chinese Checkers with Lin, or reading
the books Lin provided her with from the
homestead library. Sarah's province remained in
the servants' quarters, and she had no wish to
explore further for fear of meeting Sean and
receiving another sneering reference to her
'snooping'.

On one occasion she had gone out to the
vegetable garden at the back of the homestead,

just to get a breath of fresh air, for it was a lovely night with a full moon, and the stars just as large as she had seen on the drive to the homestead. She had not known how long she had stood there, drinking in the wonders of the night, with the lowing of the cattle in the distant pastures adding to the pastoral symphony, but then a harsh voice had broken into her reverie. 'Wear a cardigan next time. You're not in the city now. The temperatures have a habit of dropping suddenly here.'

Sarah, furious at the interruption, spat out, 'I haven't got one,' and with tears blinding her vision stumbled back into the homestead.

The next day Lin presented her with a lambswool jacket, and a far from grateful Sarah had spurned the gift. Sean Cartier had sent it, since Lin knew nothing of what had happened the previous evening; Sarah had been too upset to face even the gentle Chinese, and had gone straight to her room.

She had, during the course of that first week, tried to elicit a few facts from Lin, such as where they were, and how far was the nearest township, whether he did the shopping, and which day he went—all to no avail. The answers did not get her anywhere, and this wasn't Lin's fault. It was simply that the homestead was in the middle of nowhere. The supplies were brought in, and left at Joe's garage for collection, the nearest point from the main highway.

It was as Sarah had suspected at the start. Sean Cartier had chosen well when he had brought her here. But then he would, she thought angrily. He didn't make mistakes, and certainly not where she was concerned. She longed to see a paper, just to convince herself that somewhere in the world everyone was going on with their normal business, but here she met a blank. No papers, it seemed, were to be had, and she suspected that this again was Sean Cartier's doing. She hadn't even seen an old one, and when she remarked on this to Lin, he had placidly said that all news was gloomy, better without them. He wasn't bothered, and boss wasn't bothered either.

Sarah took exception to this bald condemnation of her profession, but held her tongue. Lin did not know that she was a journalist, and she had a feeling that in his old-fashioned way he would have been astounded had he known, and not a little disappointed in her.

Almost a week after Pauline Cook's visit to the homestead, Sarah had an accident. She had balanced herself on a spindly kitchen stool in order to reach into one of the kitchen cupboards. Like Lin, she was not tall enough to reach the higher cupboards, and she overbalanced and fell heavily on to her left shoulder.

At least it was only her shoulder that had taken the brunt of the fall, and a shaky exploration of the arm had proved that the arm was not broken. Lin, returning from doing the household chores at this point, was extremely concerned to find her sitting on the floor leaning up against the wall while she recovered her breath.

He hovered over her anxiously, and assisted her to her feet and over to a kitchen chair while he made her a hot drink. 'Boss over at Cooks',' he said worriedly. 'I can get him on the radio.'

'You'll do no such thing,' Sarah said hastily, her weakness now replaced by an abhorrence of having herself examined by that man. 'Look, I haven't broken my arm. All I've got is a bruised shoulder. It's painful now, but in a day or so I'll be okay,' she stated firmly.

She saw Lin's anxious glance at her. He wanted to believe her, but she knew what he had in mind. Had she dislocated her shoulder? Well, she was certain that she hadn't. It was painful, but not that painful. 'Look, I can move my shoulder. See?' She winced at the pain this movement produced, but it proved her point for the time being. 'He'll be furious if you haul him back for nothing,' she went on.

Lin remained unconvinced, but he promised not to put a call out for Sean's return to the homestead, and said nothing about his intentions when Sean returned later that night.

It was as much as Sarah could hope for. During the course of the day, she would somehow prove that it was not necessary for him to inform his master about the accident. No matter what it cost her that shoulder was going to make a rapid recovery!

By the time she went to her room soon after ten that evening, she was sure that she had succeeded in convincing Lin that there was nothing to worry about. She had refused to act the invalid and sit on one of the kitchen chairs while Lin prepared their lunch, and insisted on doing small chores that she was sure that she couldn't have done if she had done any serious damage to her shoulder.

Once in her room, however, she came up against the problem of removing her cotton top. As thin and light as it was, the now stiffening shoulder sent waves of pain through her as she attempted its removal.

After several tries, she gave it up. She would have to sleep in the wretched thing. Perhaps tomorrow when the bruises came out it would be more manageable.

She had just got herself in as near a comfortable position for sleep as was possible, when after a perfunctory knock, Sean was in her room.

For a moment or so she thought she was dreaming, then she snapped out of her doziness, and attempted to sit up a little too quickly for the injured shoulder. The pain made her angrier still at the way he had foisted his presence on to her.

'Lin told me you'd had a fall,' he said abruptly, before she could vent her feelings on him.

'It's nothing,' she said between her teeth. 'I told Lin to say nothing about it, and he promised,' she added indignantly.

Sean stood looking down at her from his great height, then with a purposeful stride he came towards the bed. 'Lin is my man,' he said bluntly. 'He knew better than to obey your instructions. Let's have a look at that shoulder,' he ordered brusquely, then stared down at her. 'Do you usually sleep in your day clothes?' he demanded. 'Why the hell didn't you tell me you were that short?' he said angrily. 'I thought you people always travelled prepared for stopovers.'

'We do!' Sarah replied just as angrily. 'Only I didn't come prepared for a four week stopover!' she added furiously.

To her further annoyance, Sean seemed to think this was amusing, and a brief grin flitted over his usually stern features.

He didn't have to ask which shoulder it was by the crooked way Sarah was sitting, and she had to suffer the indignity of his probing fingers around her collarbone first, then on to the shoulder-bone.

For such a big man his touch was gentle but sure, because Sarah was prepared to shout like mad if he hurt her, but to her disappointment no such display was warranted. 'You've only bruised it,' he said, after a perfunctory examination. 'Be sore for a few days,' he added, 'but nothing to worry about.'

She glared up at him. 'I could have told you that,' she said pithily. 'Now, do you mind if I get some sleep?'

'After we've made you a little more comfort-able,' he replied, and left the room before she could reply, and she was left wondering whether he would bring her a couple more pillows, or perhaps a couple of painkillers to help her sleep. Her mind rambled on; she didn't think she would need anything to make her sleep, it was taking her all her time to stay awake now, she thought drowsily, then recalling what he had said about her sleeping in her T-shirt, she gave an ironic smile. She didn't think he would have any spare nightdresses about the place. Of course, there was always one of Lin's nightshirts!

She was rudely awoken out of these amusing imaginings by the return of Sean, and her wide eyes went first to the bowl of hot liquid that he was carrying, then to the flimsy nightdress slung over his shoulders. The smell emitting from the bowl reminded her of her bygone youth when she had helped out at a local stables to pay for her riding lessons. The liniment that they had put on lame horses' forelegs had had a similar smell, but that was nothing to the indignation she felt on sight of that flimsy nightdress. If he thought——

'Just what,' she demanded dangerously, 'did you have in mind?'

Sean's blue eyes met hers. 'This will ease the soreness,' he said, indicating the bowl he put down on the bedside table, and slung the nightdress across the bed. 'I don't think I have to explain that,' he added.

'Have a stock of them, do you?' asked Sarah, taking refuge in sarcasm. She was both embarrassed and furious.

Sean's eyes glinted dangerously. 'Watch your words, my girl,' he warned her. 'You're in no position to fling out any challenges.'

'Who's challenging?' Sarah bit out. 'Well, you can leave the liniment. I'll put some on,' she added grudgingly, 'and thanks for the thought,' she tacked on. He was right, she was in no position to antagonise him.

Sean gave her a long look. 'Take that shirt off,' he ordered, as he dipped some cotton wool into the liniment.

She stared at him. 'I said I would do it,' she declared, feeling panic rise up.

Sean's blue eyes looked like chips of ice. 'Look, I'm tired. So let's get this over, shall we? How the hell can you do it? You're not a contortionist, are you? Don't tell me you're shy,' he sneered at her. 'I'm not exactly a country boy—I've been around.'

Hence the stock of flimsy nightdresses, thought a frantic Sarah; anything to take her mind off her predicament. 'I'll let Lin do it,' she replied obstinately.

Sean let out a long sigh that showed that his patience was at an end with her. 'I wouldn't dream of causing him such embarrassment,' he said through clenched teeth. 'He'd have to be blindfolded first, and that could lead to a few problems.'

They seemed to be at stalemate, but Sarah had not bargained for Sean's determination. He caught hold of the bottom of her shirt and proceeded to ease it up to her shoulders, but even in her fury, it was plain to see her pain at attempting to raise her arm.

Without more ado, Sean went over to the dressing-table and opened one of the top drawers, and after a short search emerged with a pair of nail scissors in his hand, then he strode back to the utterly miserable Sarah, who was through complaining. It was like coming up against a stone wall, and the sooner you stopped banging your head against it, the better!

She felt the cotton material give as he cut it from the back, and it was only a matter of seconds before the tattered remains of the shirt were eased from her shoulders.

It wasn't much consolation, but Sarah was glad that she still had her bra on, so at least she was still decent, but she had reckoned without Sean, who, without a by your leave, slipped the strap down from her injured shoulder, and left her feeling as if she was taking part in a strip-tease. Somewhere, she thought wildly, there should be accompanying music, only she didn't have a feather to cover herself with, she mused hysterically, as she clutched hastily at the slowly lowering strap that was about to reveal all.

Sean was dipping the cotton wool into the liniment at that point, but was not too absorbed in his task to miss this sudden action of preservation on Sarah's part. 'If you're putting on an act for my benefit, forget it,' he said angrily. 'Like me, you've been around. Trying to act the innocent cuts no ice with me. It just bores me.' He gave a swift glance about the room. The old counterpane had been changed for a soft blue one, the rickety chair replaced by an old but comfortable armchair, and the lino covered by a long blue runner carpet. 'You've fooled Lin, I see,' he commented caustically, 'and that's pretty good. I always thought he was more than shrewd.'

He dabbed on the liniment with sure practised strokes. 'But then you're good at fooling people, aren't you?' he went on, 'even wise old Lin. It just goes to show how much damage you can do.' He popped the soaked cotton wool back into the bowl, and stood up and gazed down at her. 'I suppose there's lots more Dons out there, aren't there, just panting to fall under your spell. Makes you feel good, does it, seeing a man on his knees? Well, that little pleasure will have to wait a mite longer,' he added harshly, then he walked towards the door, but looked back at her as he opened it. 'Of course,' he mused hatefully, 'it could be months before they decide to publish that find, maybe years.'

Sarah's brilliant eyes showed her feelings, and he gave a low laugh. 'What a pity it's all wasted. You could be past your prime when the all clear's given.'

She wanted to throw the bowl at him, but she knew the chances were that she would miss and leave a mess for poor Lin to clear up the following day, so she contented herself by paying Sean back in his own coin. She sent him a luring smile—as he had said, she was practised in cajolery. 'Aren't you going to help me into this lovely nightie?' she asked huskily. 'I'm practically helpless, you know,' she added temptingly.

She had the pleasure of seeing Sean's face harden, and his eyes pierced hers. 'I might take you up on that some time,' he said harshly. 'Thank your lucky stars that you're out of action for the time being,' and he slammed the door behind him as he stamped out of the room.

Sarah sat blinking in amazement at her audacity. How could she have been so stupid! If he had taken her up on her offer she would have died of shame! She eased herself down into the bed. Already the shoulder had lost its stiffness. Whatever liniment he had used, it was working, and by the next day should be hardly noticeable.

Her eyelids drooped as she felt sleep stealing

over her. Why on earth had she taunted him like
that? she thought drowsily. How stupid could
you get? Yet somehow she had known that she
was safe. He had put enough distance between
them the last time his feelings got the better of
him, hadn't he? No, she concluded, with a
drowsy sigh, he might be attracted to her, but his
pride would always win the day. On this
comfortable thought, she fell asleep.

The next morning her shoulder was so much
better that she was able to dress without too
much discomfort. Purplish blue patches were
appearing at the top of her arm, and this was all
to the good, she thought, as she slipped on the
blouse of her silk suit. Apart from Martha's
revealing T-shirt, that she couldn't possibly wear
until she had stitched up the front, she had no
option but to wear the blouse, that had not taken
kindly to washing, owing to the fact that it
needed special treatment, and was a mass of
creases. There was also the salient fact that it was
meant for more fancy occasions than a stay in the
wilds. Sarah had been in attendance at a
prizegiving ceremony when the summons had
come through for this assignment, and had only
been able to dash back to the flat to pick up her
overnight case, that was always kept at the ready
for such occasions.

She sighed as she surveyed the limp wrinkled
patches on the blouse. If only she had known—
The first thing on the agenda now was a needle
and thread. She ought to have seen to it before,
she told herself, as she made her way down to the
kitchen for breakfast.

Lin's half worried glance at her on her arrival in the kitchen, turned into a pleased smile when she said airily, 'All right, I forgive you. I hadn't thought you might get into trouble if you didn't tell the boss.'

On his enquiry on how the shoulder was, she was able to give a favourable report. The stiffness had gone, she told him.

After breakfast, she was mystified by Lin's solemn, 'Missy come with me,' and followed him warily out of the kitchen and through to the main section of the homestead.

For obvious reasons, she hung back from what she was certain was going to be a confrontation with Sean, and sensing her reluctance, Lin said simply, 'Boss says you need shirts. We go and see what's what.'

Sarah's eyebrows rose, as she wondered whose shirts would be offered. Lin's or Sean's? Lin's would fit her better than his boss's. On the other hand, Sean's shirts would make her a nice mini-dress, although she wasn't too sure that Lin would approve, she thought lightheartedly, her spirits somewhat lightened after her fears of meeting Sean had been dispelled.

To her amazement, the room Lin took her to was as feminine a boudoir as she had ever seen. Soft lilacs and pinks blended together, with deep purple drapes at the wide windows, and a matching velvet counterpane on the splendid divan. Lovely watercolour pictures hung on the Regency striped walls, and on either side of the fitted dressing-table unit were deep fitted ward-robes, where Lin was obviously headed, followed a little reluctantly by Sarah, her feet sinking into the deep pile of a lilac carpet.

There couldn't have been a greater comparison from this suite with the room that Sarah had been given, for it had its own en-suite shower room, that she caught sight of through an open door, as tastefully fitted out as the room she was in, and she could now understand Lin's embarrassment on learning where she was to be billeted.

However, had she been given a choice she would cheerfully have plumped for the quarters she was in, rather than these ultra-luxurious surroundings, particularly under the circumstances of her presence at the homestead. She wasn't a guest, just a tramp Sean Cartier had wanted to teach a lesson.

Lin slid one of the wardrobe doors back and disclosed shelves with several feminine articles on them, among them light blouses and warm jumpers. 'Boss says take what you want,' he invited her smilingly.

Sarah stared at the clothes. They were not off-the-peg articles, but costly garments, and she was horrified at the thought of raiding someone else's wardrobe, and moved back away from the wardrobe as if she had been caught stealing. 'I'd rather not,' she said firmly, convinced that these clothes belonged to one of Sean Cartier's women, and she would rather wear Martha's T-shirt, deep V or no deep V!

Lin surveyed her solemnly. 'Missy Kathy not mind,' he said softly in his sing-song voice.

'But I do,' Sarah stated flatly. 'No matter about what Missy Kathy likes. If you could let me have a needle and thread, I can manage with what I've got,' she said firmly.

Lin's expression was quite comical, and if Sarah hadn't been so put out by the fact that Sean Cartier expected her to wear his women's clothes, she might have been amused. As it was, she was coldly furious.

'No understand,' Lin said patiently. 'Missy Kathy boss's sister. Now Missy Bandaman. Comes for break from city sometimes. No come for some time,' he added urgingly.

Sarah could not understand why Lin's words gave her such a lift of the heart, but they did, and she wasn't about to seek an explanation. However, Mrs Bandaman—all women, it seemed, were 'Missy' to Lin—would not feel at all happy at someone wearing her clothes. 'I'm not all that badly off for clothes, Lin,' she said cheerfully, 'and I'm not expecting to stay all that long,' and she turned to leave.

She had reckoned without Lin's persistence, for he stood his ground, and pulled out an ace that he had apparently kept up his sleeve that was somewhat reminiscent of his master. 'Boss angry with Lin if Missy doesn't use clothes,' he said simply, managing to look very worried indeed.

Sarah stared at him, trying to read those enigmatic eyes of his, then sighed. He could be right, she thought. That man gave orders and expected them to be carried out, and recalling how angry he had been when he thought that she had been sleeping in her day clothes, she thought it was quite possible that he would take it out on Lin.

With the utmost reluctance, she selected three plain blouses, and a warm jumper, and with a pleased smile Lin gathered them up, then directed her attention to the drawers of the dressing-table, with a 'Missy find more in there,' then with the discretion that was typical of him he silently left her.

As expected, she found dainty silk underwear, again of the best quality, and not too happily she selected only the minimum of what she would need, telling herself that she would replace them, as soon as the all clear was sounded, and refusing to dwell on Sean's dark hints of a long stay.

Lin appeared again when she had closed the drawers, and escorted her back to the kitchen quarters with the loot, as she regarded it, and she carried it off to her room.

CHAPTER EIGHT

A DAY later, Lin's bright and confident forecast that Missy Bandaman would not be likely to pay them a visit suffered a severe setback with the arrival of that lady.

Again, it was Lin who first heard the arrival of a vehicle and with a nod of certainty said to Sarah, 'Missy Pauline,' as he left the kitchen with Sean's mid-morning coffee tray.

However, he very shortly returned for an extra cup, his normally calm demeanour showing some agitation. 'Missy Bandaman,' he said.

Sarah, glancing down at the beautiful lawn blouse she was wearing, left the room and made her way to her own room. She was taking no chances of being found with the goods on her, and from past experience she could not rely on being safe in the kitchen!

She was halfway along the passage when she heard a female voice demanding, 'Who is she, Sean? I met Pauline yesterday at the Deckmans', and she told me you'd got some blonde up here, helping out in the kitchen. Some drifter you'd picked up in Darwin, she gleaned. Lin's managed perfectly well all these years without help, so what's going on? It's not like you to fall for a hard luck story.'

Sarah grimaced as she sped on to her room to change. So Pauline Cook hadn't accepted Sean's explanation for her presence in the homestead, if he had bothered to give her one, and knowing him this was unlikely. He did precisely what he wanted to do, girl-friend or no girl-friend, she thought sourly as she reached her room and proceeded to remove the blouse.

One look at her creased silk blouse, now more creased, because she had tucked it back into her overnight case in the mistaken belief that she would not have to wear it again, made her fish out Martha's T-shirt. Beggars could not be choosers, she told herself as she slipped it on, and made the mistake of glancing in the mirror at her reflection, then wished she hadn't. The wretched front was even lower than she had thought it was, and made her decide to stay put in the hope that Mrs Bandaman would make an early departure. She had no intention of giving credence to Pauline Cook's spiteful comment of her being a drifter.

However, there was no peace for the wicked, and Sarah thought that she must be very wicked, by the way things had a nasty habit of backfiring on her, for after a tentative knock at her door by Lin, she was told that boss wanted to see her.

Sarah saw Lin's startled look at the T-shirt, but by now he must be getting inured to shocks, she presumed, by his swift recovery and polite waiting position giving her no option but to accompany him.

They went through the kitchen, and towards the front of the house, and after turning a corner came to the entrance hall that Sarah had only seen once since her arrival, and had not been given chance to linger in.

As in the bedroom suite that she had seen a day ago, no expense had been spared. The hall carpet was as deep as the bedroom one, only in more sober colours that echoed the deep rich pine of the hall furniture, and a large gilt mirror hung on one side, giving the area an awesomely roomy appearance, while the steady ticking of a tall beautifully ornate grandfather clock added to Sarah's apprehension, that was somewhat underlined by catching a glimpse of herself in the mirror as they passed.

Lin tapped on a door on the right of the hall, and without more ado, Sarah found herself ushered into a room as tastefully furnished as one would expect from the small glimpses of the homestead's main quarters that she had so far seen.

Her gaze, however, went directly to a tall, slender woman standing next to Sean on the rich hearthrug in front of an ornate fireplace.

She felt, rather than saw, Sean's quick gaze at her apparel, and for a moment it appeared to have taken the wind out of his sails, as it was his sister who spoke first.

'Good gracious! What are you doing here?' she demanded.

Sarah blinked and looked at Sean. 'You know her?'. he asked.

'Of course I do,' Mrs Bandaman replied airily. 'We always know the press. You're on the *Daily*, aren't you?' she said to Sarah. 'I don't suppose you remember me, but we always invite the press to our annual conferences, and we had a very nice write-up to get that maternity unit we battled for,' she added happily, then coming back to the present, looked at her brother. 'But what's the press doing here? Have I missed out on a story?' she enquired.

'Sort of,' Sean replied grimly. 'I'm afraid she got a bit too nosey, and found out something we can't afford to have published.'

Kathy Bandaman stared at her brother. 'Really?' she said, and her bewildered glance went from Sean to Sarah. 'Well, I presume this has something to do with your work,' she said after an appreciable pause, now directing her attention back to Sean, 'but surely——' she broke off, lost for words.

Sarah decided to end all speculation. 'I'm being kept here against my will, Mrs Bandaman,' she said quietly. 'I've given my word to Mr Cartier that I won't divulge anything I've learned, not until he gives the word, that is, but he doesn't care to believe me.'

Sean sent her a murderous look, but having now got started, Sarah was not about to give up, 'Look, if I signed a statement to that effect, it ought to be good enough, oughtn't it? It stands to reason I'll lose my job if I renege on it,' she argued plausibly.

Kathy Bandaman looked hard at her brother. 'Is this true?' she demanded. 'Are you deliberately keeping her here? After she's given her word that she wouldn't print anything that you considered confidential?'

'She's not getting the chance,' Sean replied flatly.

Sarah gave a loud sigh. 'So you see,' she said angrily, 'I'm supposed to stay until they publish——' she stopped short here; she had almost said 'the strike', and Sean was angry enough with her already without her adding to his fury. She had already sent whatever plausible excuse he had ready to give his sister for her presence in the homestead up in flames, but it was now or never for her.

Mrs Bandaman sat down slowly on one of the fireside chairs. It was plain that she was still bewildered. 'I can't say how sorry I am about this,' she said sympathetically to Sarah. 'I'm afraid I don't know your name?'

'Sarah Helm,' Sarah supplied, with a sinking feeling that she had lost out. She was there for keeps, she thought miserably.

'Oh do sit down,' Mrs Bandaman said quickly. 'The least we can do is to make you comfortable.'

Sarah did not think that this was a good idea; she did not fancy Sean gazing down at her, from his great height, for obvious reasons; she was uncomfortable enough as it was.

'Sarah Helm,' Kathy Bandaman repeated slowly. 'I've heard that name before, but where——?' She glanced at her brother.

Sean had no intention of enlightening her, and Sarah knew why. His sister would see the real reason for his adamant refusal to let her go.

'Don!' Mrs Bandaman exclaimed, and looked back at Sarah. 'Were you——?'

Sarah's eyes went to Sean's grim face, as she nodded. There was no point in lying, and she waited to hear what she was sure was going to be a long bitter tirade on the subject—but she was in for a surprise.

'Oh, my dear, you don't seem to be having much luck with our family, do you?' Mrs Bandaman said sympathetically. 'You must have felt awful about what happened.'

Sean gave a derisive snort. 'Considering she broke the engagement off the day before it happened, I should hardly think so,' he said harshly.

His sister stared at him. 'Well, that just goes to show how sensible she was,' she stated firmly. 'No doubt she found him out,' she added flatly.

Sarah could hardly believe her ears. At last, here was someone actually on her side!

'You never liked him, did you?' Sean accused his sister.

'No,' Kathy replied promptly. 'And neither would you have done. The same went for Granny Worthing—you didn't know the half of it. You were away on your travels most of the time, so you really couldn't see what he was like. The same went for poor old Granny. He used to make the odd visit to her now and again. He had great expectations there, you know.' Her dark eyes went to her brother. 'The fact that you were such good pals in your youth would bias you, but I knew what Don was like,' she said grimly. 'I could have put you right on several things if I'd chosen to when I was in my teens.'

Sarah was beginning to feel uncomfortable. This was family business, and no concern of hers.

It was evident that Sean felt the same, as he said harshly, 'Would you mind leaving us?'

Sarah didn't mind, and promptly made her departure before Kathy could request her to stay, as she had been about to do, Sarah was sure, but she did not give her time to voice her request.

Going back to the kichen, she gladly accepted the coffee Lin had got ready for her. If he was curious about the outcome of the interview, he did not show it, but was more concerned about the fact of whether Mrs Bandaman would be staying for dinner, and a rearrangement of the menu.

While Lin fussed about the menu, Sarah's thoughts were on the ensuing events likely to arise from Sean's sister's revelations, and she felt a spurt of hope surge through her.

Sean had not been inclined to believe her, but she was sure that he would believe his sister, no matter how much it went against the grain. Therefore it stood to reason that he would have to release her, she told herself happily, and she cheerily started to help Lin prepare the lunch.

A lunch she found, to her consternation, that she was invited to partake with Sean and his sister, on Kathy's insistence, it seemed, as Sean's attitude towards her was just as unbending as it had been before.

Not that this surprised Sarah. She knew how it felt to have one's balloon burst. He could no longer treat her as a second class citizen, but she was soon to find that she had miscalculated her man.

After a few desultory attempts at conversation, hard going, because Sarah was not inclined to be forthcoming, and Sean giving barely polite remarks on whatever subject his sister tried to introduce, Kathy came to the point. 'Look,' she

said to Sean, 'will you let me take Sarah back to
the Deckmans' with me? She must be bored to
death out here. She's given her promise not to do
anything about whatever it is that's so confidential——'

That was as far as Sean let her get. 'Sorry,' he
said abruptly. 'It's still no go. She's staying here
where I can keep an eye on her.'

'For goodness' sake——!' his sister began, then
was quelled by the look in Sean's eyes, and gave
an exasperated sigh as she turned to Sarah. 'I'm
sorry, Sarah,' she said slowly. 'He doesn't trust
anyone, it seems.'

That was the end of the matter as far as Sarah's
imminent release went, and she could have
screamed with frustration. It was doubly hard for
her to sit calmly after lunch and try to hold a cosy
chat with Kathy Bandaman while Sean took
himself off to check on the tyres of his sister's
borrowed car, as she had mentioned the possibility of having a slow puncture.

All of which was untrue, Kathy confessed
confidentially to Sarah as soon as Sean had left
them. 'Julia would have fifty fits if she had heard
what I said about her new Simca that she'd been
good enough to put at my disposal,' she had
added, 'but it simply is not possible to have a
conversation with the pair of you glaring at each
other. You mustn't let him bully you, you know,'
she advised Sarah. 'The trouble is he's too used
to having his own way, and he's probably got it in
for you over Don, but I think I've scotched that
nonsense.' She frowned. 'I'm afraid we're not
going to get him to change his mind about your

coming back with me, but as soon as all this is over, you must come and stay with me, and give me a chance to make up for all this.'

Sarah thanked her solemnly, but made no promise. Once this was over, she devoutly hoped to be able to keep out of the Cartier family's way for the rest of time.

'Good gracious!' exclaimed Kathy suddenly, 'what about your people? If I know Sean's high-handed way of managing things, that wouldn't occur to him,' she said worriedly, 'and I've been so muddleheaded since I found out the reason for your presence here that it didn't occur to me either,' she added apologetically.

Sarah regretfully assured her that she had no living relations. If she had had, no doubt she wouldn't be in this fix. Someone would have made a move to rescue her.

'But your paper?' Kathy asked. 'Do they still think you're on the assignment?'

'In a way,' Sarah replied, not willing to tell Sean's sister of the way her brother had explained her absence.

'Well, it's all highly unsatisfactory,' Kathy said indignantly. 'I have to leave shortly, and I don't want to leave you here. Look, if you grab your things and just go and sit in the car, there won't be anything that Sean can do about it, will there?' she suggested brightly.

'I wouldn't bet on it!' said Sean as he strode into the room at that point. 'Of course I've no wish to manhandle Miss Helm, but if she does attempt any such move I shall be forced to adopt such tactics.'

His sister looked shocked. 'Sean, you wouldn't!' she exclaimed unbelievingly.

Sean's hard gaze went from Sarah back to his sister. 'Try me,' he said quietly, then added in a conversational voice, 'I could let her go with you, and have her picked up by the Security people, but somehow I don't think either of you would care for that.'

As he had known, this bald statement quelled whatever rebellion Sarah and his sister planned, and in the pregnant silence that followed, he went on airily, 'One thing I'm curious about, is how you knew the name of Don's fiancée. I only discovered that she was a small-time reporter who'd gone on to higher things. Don appeared to have kept his private life close to his chest.'

'Granny Worthing's effects,' Kathy replied, still partially stunned at the thought of getting involved with the forces of the law. 'There was no one else to take them,' she said. 'Not that I bothered at the time. I just put them in the attic, always meaning to go through them, and throw out what wasn't suitable to keep.' She took a deep breath, and made a valiant effort to concentrate on the topic. 'We're doing a play and it's in the twenties period, and it occurred to me that Granny might have some old dresses we could use, so I opened the trunks, and while I was at it, I thought I might as well go through all the stuff. I found a letter from Don telling her that he'd just got engaged and giving her the girl's name,' she faltered here, and gave up trying to get interested in anything else but Sean's startling disclosure. 'Are you serious about getting Sarah arrested?' she demanded.

Sean gave her a pitying look. 'I happen to like my job,' he said grimly, 'and in spite of Miss Helm's obvious attractions, I can assure you that once the all clear is given, I shall speed her on her way so fast, she'll wonder what hit her,' he promised harshly. 'Now you'd better be on your way. I suppose you've got to call on the Cooks? Well, there's nothing wrong with those tyres, you've probably been driving too fast. The vehicle has to be run in at a gentle pace, remember—and not a word about anything we've just been discussing, not unless you want to see me out of a job,' he emphasised.

Kathy nodded slowly, then picked up her handbag, and with a glance at Sarah said unhappily, 'For goodness' sake, what do I tell Pauline?'

'Tell her I've got a crush on the girl,' he replied lightly, his blue eyes rested on Sarah's indignant features with a mocking light in them.

'Sean, really!' his sister exclaimed. 'You know perfectly well how she feels about you,' she scolded, 'although I'd rather she set her sights elsewhere. A little of Pauline goes a long way,' she ended sadly, and with a little wave at Sarah, she left.

Sarah, still fuming at Sean's sarcastic reference to her, actually cementing Pauline Cook's suspicions that she was a drifter that he had picked up, left the lounge for the kitchen quarters. She preferred Lin's company any day to that pompous individual's!

As far as she was concerned, there was only one bright spot on the horizon, and that was that her

stay was not indefinite, and sooner or later she
would be sped on her way, as he had stated. She
could only hope that it would be sooner, rather
than later—and hadn't he piled it on! she thought
furiously, as she started to help Lin with the
washing up. As if he would lose his job! She
didn't believe that for a moment. Sean Cartier
would go to any lengths to get his way.

Whatever disclosures his sister had made about
Don's past had not made the slightest difference
to his behaviour towards her. By now, she
thought angrily, she ought to have been receiving
his apology, but she could no more imagine that
than she could imagine her freedom at that point
in time.

In this, however, she was shortly proved
wrong, for as she sat playing Chinese Checkers
with Lin that evening, Sean demanded her
presence in the lounge, and for one hopeful
minute Sarah wondered if the all clear had been
given.

In the event, this hope was soon dispelled, as
his first words were, 'I suppose I owe you an
apology,' given in a stiff unbending manner, that
didn't sound at all apologetic to the annoyed and
disappointed Sarah.

'It's a little late for that, isn't it?' Sarah replied
angrily, 'and I can't think why you're bothering.
You certainly laid it on thick with your sister,
didn't you? All that nonsense about losing your
job, which I don't believe for one minute. Just as
I've never believed in this wonderful find you're
supposed to have made. It stands to reason that it
would have been made public by now. No,' she

went on, unheeding the glints in Sean's eyes that should have been a warning signal if she hadn't been so incensed, 'you're just working out a private vendetta. You wouldn't listen to me, but you were only too ready to listen to the lies Charles Ashley told you about my style of life. Well, that's his way, it's certainly not mine. Not that I care what you believe. I just want out,' she ended fiercely.

'Now you just listen to me, you little wildcat,' Sean said harshly. 'Firstly, you can disabuse yourself of the fact that I'm on a crusade where you're concerned. It's perfectly true that I don't care for your profession, but that's your business. I'll now give you a few facts about my business. What I told you about the 'C' factor was true. If you had a little more intelligence you would have realised that a strike like that has to be doubly checked, and that's precisely what's happening now. All those figures you typed out, all the specimens of soil, strata levels, are only half of it. We've been looking for it for over three years now, and I'm pretty sure we've found it, but I don't have the last word, not on something as important as this. Believe me, when it is confirmed, it won't be just our press that will flock for information, but the world press. We're not the only ones that have been looking for it, but we've won the race. And if you think I'd let anyone put that in jeopardy, then you'd better think again,' he advised her harshly.

Sarah realised the futility of going on with the argument, and made her way to the door.

'And you can put on something decent,' he

shouted at her before she left. 'You've no excuse now for going about looking like a wanton!'

Sarah was beyond replying, and she closed the door behind her with a firm click that somehow suggested her feelings about that last statement of his, then she went straight to her room.

Once there she sat down on her bed, willing herself not to give way to the utter desolation in her heart and weep it all out of her system.

She simply would not allow that despicable man to get the better of her, she told herself, biting on her lower lip to gain her composure. She had no doubt at all that what he had just told her was true, and it seemed that she had been deceiving herself all along the line as to his real reason for denying her her freedom.

Her fingers clutched the bright blue bedspread. Was that the kind of woman she had turned into? she thought bewilderedly. Had her head been turned to the extent that she had lost all sense of proportion and now suspected every man of having designs on her? Was she the very type of woman Sean Cartier had accused her of being?

Not once, she thought miserably, had she considered the importance of his work; that side of it had never occurred to her. She had been too busy seeing herself as a maligned female who happened to be attractive to the opposite sex. In her eyes she had credited her captor with all the human failings of his gender, and had well deserved the setdown she had just been given.

At this point a tiny voice inside her reminded her that he could have sent her off with the rest of the reporters, but had chosen to keep her there. He had also, that small voice went on ruthlessly, made a point of telling her about the find—why?

Her eyes opened wide as she got the answer. She had threatened to sue him, hadn't she, and he had trumped her master card with an ace. As she had suspected he was not the type of man to make mistakes. Everything he did was done on purpose.

All this time he had been amusing himself at her expense, she thought angrily, now coming back to a healthy dislike of him, as she recalled the way his eyes had mocked her when he had told his sister to tell Pauline that he had got a crush on her.

How he must have regretted having to use that information to keep himself out of the courts, Sarah thought. The only real slip he had made was in letting his personal feelings get the better of him, determined to exact some form of punishment from her, and if she hadn't been such a stupid ninny as to tell him she was going to sue him for denying her her freedom, he wouldn't have had to resort to such drastic action.

No wonder he had met that bus from the National Park, and every other bus, if she hadn't been on that! It must have given him a few bad moments, and for that at least she was glad; everything else had gone his way.

The following morning's bright sunshine did nothing to help lighten Sarah's spirits, but only served to make her feel even more abandoned to the outside world. She wished she could wander in the homestead grounds, but there was Lin to

consider. There was no doubt that he had been
instructed to keep an eye on her—not that there
was anywhere that she could go to gain her
freedom, and she did not want to put Lin's
vigilance to the test by wandering off out of sight,
because he would certainly contact his boss,
wherever he was, for Sarah had heard the Land
Rover starting up shortly after she had got down
to breakfast.

At eleven-thirty, she was amazed to hear that
she was wanted on the telephone. 'Missy
Bandaman want to talk to you,' Lin told her, and
took her to a room beyond the lounge that served
as a study, that had a two-way radio transmission
set, and as Sarah had never used one before, Lin
showed her how to flick the switch over to hear the
message, to flick it back before she replied, and to
speak into the small microphone in front of her.

'Sarah?' Kathy Bandaman's voice floated
clearly over the line. 'When are you leaving? I
was due to go today, but I'll stay over and pick
you up around tennish tomorrow, if that's all right
with you. I don't think Sean will have any
objection. It will save him a journey, won't it?'

Sarah stared down at the set in front of her. 'Go
where?' she asked, and at the ensuing silence
realised that she had not switched over. 'Go
where?' she repeated, when she had pushed the
switch over for Kathy to hear her.

'Haven't you seen the paper?' asked Kathy.
'It's front page news. Your paper seems to have
scooped the lot! Sean's got a terrific write-up.
He's got the credit, of course, for the find,' she
went on happily, 'and he's going to be too busy

with the press from now on to worry about you. Tell him I'll pick you up. Isn't it exciting?' she babbled on, and then the line went dead.

Sarah went back to the kitchen in a kind of dream. She couldn't really believe it was all over. 'Mrs Bandaman is going to pick me up tomorrow, Lin,' she said, still trying to come to terms with the news. 'It seems that your boss has become famous overnight,' she went on. 'No doubt he'll have to leave for the city himself soon.'

Lin looked up from the lunch that he was preparing for them. 'Boss not like press,' he said simply. 'Lin thinks that's why he went off this morning. No want any more calls. Home address not known, you see, boss been in papers before.'

Sarah looked hard at him. 'Are you telling me he knew it would be in the papers today?' she asked.

Lin nodded. 'Got call soon after Missy Bandaman left. Told me to say he was out. Missy Bandaman different,' he added simply.

Sarah stared at him while she digested this news. In that case, she reasoned, he must have known that the news had been released when he gave her that set-down the previous evening! Of all the—just wait until he got back!

CHAPTER NINE

SARAH's fury had to wait, however, until the early evening when Sean did put in an appearance. By that time she had calmed herself down to a cold simmering anger. She had also changed into 'something decent' and now wore another of Kathy's blouses.

As the hours had gone by during the day, the more certain she was that Sean was at the Cook station, making up for lost time where Pauline was concerned, no doubt, and probably telling her the whole story. Not that it mattered to her, she told herself, pulling herself up sharply when she saw where these thoughts were leading her.

There was no accounting for taste. If Pauline Cook wanted Sean Cartier for a husband, then Sarah felt sorry for her. She had obviously only seen one side of him, the side that was charming and indolent, and had no idea how ruthless he could be in getting his own way.

Shortly after dinner that evening Sarah, refusing to wait until he deigned to see her, sought him out for the show down, and found him just finishing his coffee in the lounge.

'Congratulations,' she said, in a tight hard voice. 'I noted that you didn't see fit to inform me that the news of the strike had been released to the press.'

Sean's blue eyes regarded her lazily, taking in

the smart blouse, and the high flush of indignation on her cheeks. 'What's the hurry?' he drawled maddeningly. 'I thought you were settling down nicely. You get on all right with Lin, don't you?' He looked away from her and studied the silver coffee pot. 'I suppose it has been a bit cramped for you, being confined to the homestead. No reason now, of course, for you to keep within bounds. We've got around two hundred acres here, and it includes a small creek. I could loan a couple of mounts from the Cooks, I presume you do ride? We'd only have a couple of weeks before the weather turned—not that we get it as bad as they do further up north, but it does curtail outings.'

Sarah stared at him. Did he really think she was fool enough to fall for that? Here he was, offering her—what was he offering her? A little dalliance, that's what it was. He wasn't intending to go back to the city, that much was obvious. He couldn't be bothered to run her back to Darwin, and had come up with an idea of killing two birds with one stone. For a couple of weeks of his charming company, she was supposed to forget his earlier treatment of her. An echo of something he had said to her at the start of their acquaintance came to mind at that point. 'You'll never know how I feel about you.' Sarah took a deep breath. She did know! She knew only too well, and she wasn't about to make a fool of herself falling into the trap.

'That's very kind of you,' she managed to get out civilly, although she did not feel very civil, and would have preferred to resort to plain speaking, 'but Mrs Bandaman is picking me up tomorrow. She was kind enough to remember me when she saw the paper this morning,' laying great emphasis on the 'remember' bit, and gratified to see Sean's eyes narrow in annoyance.

'I thought she was due to leave the Deckmans today,' he replied, telling Sarah all she had wanted to know. That was why he hadn't said anything to her earlier, or his sister either. With no immediate help to get her off the property, Sarah would again have been at the mercy of Sean Cartier's discretion.

'So she said, when she spoke to me on the air this morning,' Sarah replied, feeling a lift of spirits at the thought that at last she had got the better of him. 'But she decided to stay over to give me a lift out. She mentioned that you'd be too busy fending off the press to bother about me, so it's worked out fine, hasn't it?' she finished brightly, and turned to go, having no wish to push her luck.

'Looking forward to the bright lights again?' Sean's harsh voice halted her before she reached the door.

Sarah's brows lifted in surprise at this sudden attack. Now he was reverting back to normal, and she might as well give him his money's worth. 'Of course!' she got out, adding for good measure, 'And all those cosy dinner dates and dubious proposals. As you say, I've missed them!'

That should have been her exit, but Sean had other ideas and he covered the distance between them with a look of fury on his face that completely erased the simpering smile Sarah had conjured up to match her words, and was now replaced with a startled one. He was going to murder her, she thought.

The next minute she was in his arms and being kissed with a ferocity that hardly helped to subdue those earlier fears of hers.

If one could die by being almost totally eclipsed by a man's arms, and given no breathing space by hard lips set only on punishment, then she was being murdered, she thought weakly, and in the midst of it all, she treacherously thought it wasn't a bad way to go out, because she desperately wanted to respond to those searching lips of his, and throw caution to the winds, but her pride saw her through.

When he released her, she was weak but determined to hold out against· him. 'Thanks for the d-demonstration,' she got out breathlessly, but to her horror her eyes filled with tears, and not trusting herself to say any more, she was beyond it anyway, she hurried out of the room.

'I'm free, I'm free!' she kept repeating once she had got to her room, feeling a dire need to stiffen herself up with the thought, and not allow any other thoughts to take over. Tomorrow I'm on my way, and this time there's going to be no hiccups. It's going to be wonderful, back on the job again. To be able to please myself what I do, where I go.

Sarah was still convincing herself of how great everything was going to be as she fell asleep that night, and refused to try to understand why she did not feel as overjoyed as she should have at the prospect of freedom.

Up bright and early the next morning, she was still haunted by that unaccountable depression, that had been trying to take hold of her since the previous evening, but was slightly cheered by the prospect that Sean Cartier was not a man to give in quite so easily. It was plain that he had got it all worked out that she should stay on at the homestead and provide him with some amusement while he dodged the newshounds.

In her mind's eye she pictured him striding into the kitchen, having already been on the air to his sister to tell her that he would see to Miss Helm's departure himself, and tell her not to bother to make the journey. He would enjoy telling Sarah that.

Some people, she told herself, didn't believe in taking no for an answer; she would just have to spell it out to him. It wasn't often that he lost out, but he had met his match in Sarah Helm, she told herself proudly.

In the event, no such fine display on her part was called for, for Lin was washing up Sean's breakfast dishes when Sarah got down to the kitchen. 'Boss off early. Meeting bigwigs in city,' he commented in his dry way.

Sarah experienced a variety of feelings at this news. After all that smooth talk Sean had given her about spending two weeks on vacation! And all the time he had known of this meeting! She drew in a deep breath. It had just been an excuse for keeping her chained to the homestead on the pretence of enjoying a flirtation with her.

Thank goodness she had had the sense to turn him down, for it had obviously altered his plans.

Now she could see the way he had planned it. After her capitulation to his deadly charms, he would have casually mentioned some time during the next day that he had been called back to the city, and she would have got stuck there until he recalled her existence!

A nasty thought then assailed her. 'Mrs Bandaman's still picking me up, isn't she?' she asked Lin anxiously.

Lin looked surprised. 'Boss said Missy Bandaman come for you,' he said.

Even so, Sarah couldn't feel easy in her mind until Kathy Bandaman actually drew up in front of the homestead, and she was installed in the car, and after a kindly farewell to Lin, and almost bursting into tears at his confident, 'Missy come again,' prediction, they were off.

'I don't know how to thank you, Mrs Bandaman,' Sarah said quickly, to stop herself dwelling on Lin's hopeful but definitely wrong forecast.

'Oh, do call me Kathy,' Mrs Bandaman said. 'I'm only too pleased to be able to help. It was through Pauline really that I knew about you. It's not like Sean to burden himself with a stray female, less still take one to the homestead. It's a kind of a haven. No entertaining, no unexpected visitors, not unless you count Pauline, and she wouldn't have known that Sean was back if it hadn't been for old Joe at the garage,' Kathy added.

Sarah wondered if 'old Joe' had got the rough edge of Sean's tongue as Lin had surmised he would. For her part, she was devoutly grateful to him. It had certainly put the cat among the pigeons as far as Sean Cartier's plans were concerned.

Sarah saw that they were now coming on to a highway. 'You must think me dense,' she said, 'but I've no idea where I am, or where we're heading.'

Kathy's mouth twisted wryly. 'Typical Sean!' she commented. 'Well, we're about thirty miles away from Pine Creek. That's where the Deckmans live, and where I've been staying. I've been promising to visit for years, and when Luke, my husband, had to go off to Newcastle on business, I grabbed the opportunity. It was now or next year—the wet's on the way, and it can make travel uncomfortable. We've got three hours ahead of us to get to Darwin, and it was good of Julia to loan me her car again. Her son works in Darwin, and he'll pick it up from the airport. It's so much better than public transport, isn't it?' she mused cheerfully.

Sarah agreed with her, although she wouldn't have minded using Shanks's pony, if it meant her freedom!

'Oh, I've brought along the paper for you to see,' Kathy said, 'it's on the back seat,' and Sarah leant back and picked it up. 'As you see, you've been credited with the scoop,' Kathy went on. 'Still, you're used to seeing yourself in print, aren't you, and I hope it makes up for everything,' she added kindly.

Sarah's eyes were on the large double spaced headline of her paper that stated boldly, 'STRIKE OF THE CENTURY!' and went on with the caption underneath that read 'by our special correspondent, Sarah Helm.'

Sarah's first thought was for the other papers, who must have been chewing nails, and had had to wait for the evening edition to follow the story up. She could imagine the dark looks she would get from her erstwhile companions, and she wouldn't find herself too popular for a while. Her second thoughts were very different. How come she had got the credit for the scoop? Sean had kept his promise to Eddie, obviously, but there had been no need to highlight her part in it. Had Eddie made a point of signing her off in fine flourish, in gratitude for the scoop?

Her eyes scanned the fine print below that set out in scientific terms the value of the find. The more she read, the more indignant she became. Eddie had no right to put her name to work as detailed as this; she had had her share of scoops in the past, but she had earned them, and had no wish to take credit for something she had not done. She gave an exasperated sigh and laid the paper down on her knees.

Kathy took her eyes off the road to look at her. 'Something wrong?' she asked.

Sarah lifted an arm and then let it fall on the paper again. 'It's just not my work,' she said, 'and strange as it seems, I'm averse to claiming credit that belongs elsewhere. This——' she picked up the paper again, 'why, it's all scientific! It would take a boffin to understand it properly, let alone report on it!'

Kathy grinned. 'Oh, is that all? Well, that's easily explained. It would have been Sean's work, wouldn't it? I mean, he would have spelled it all out for them. It's not like him, I admit. He's got a thing about the press. It dates back some time. A brilliant professor of his was hounded by them—a meek and mild man, who was on to something, but was unwise enough to presume that certain remarks he had made alluded only to his hopes, and not to certainty. It was blazoned in all the papers, and would have been fine if later experiments hadn't proved the contrary, and he was made to look an honour-chasing sensation-hunter. Sadly, he became a recluse after that. One has to be so careful, you see,' she ended.

There was silence while Sarah considered this news, her eyes now on the busy highway. It helped to explain some of Sean Cartier's prejudice, but not all.

'Of course,' Kathy went on, as she skilfully overtook a heavy goods wagon, 'I shouldn't be surprised if it hadn't been Sean's idea to give the credit to you, either. He's not very good at apologising, in case you hadn't noticed,' she added with a grin at Sarah.

'I see——' Sarah said darkly, and now that it had been put to her, she did see. It would be typical of him. She was to be sent back with a feather in her cap. He had been so sure that she would grab the opportunity of revelling in the glory such a report would bring her.

She swallowed. Thank you for nothing, Sean Cartier! she thought furiously. I want no hand-outs from you. Now, or any time in the future, thank you very much!

The miles went by, and by signposts on the

way Sarah saw that they were on the Stuart Highway. She tried to keep up a flow of small talk with Kathy, but found it hard going, and sensing her mood, Kathy concentrated on her driving.

She had been so full of plans for what she would do once she had got free of that despicable man's domination that it now came as a shock to her that all she wanted was to spend some time on her own. It was amazing really, considering how much time she had had to spend whiling away the hours in the camp, longing for just this chance to get back to civilisation, but now that it had actually arrived she felt lost and uncertain of herself.

It would be all right once she was back in familiar surroundings, she told herself stoutly. It was not surprising that she should feel this way. For years she had been mistress of her own fate, pleasing herself what she did, accepting or rejecting the numerous invitations that came her way, but never getting involved emotionally. She had become adept at handling any situation that looked like getting out of hand, and would simply not be available the next time a certain individual called.

Her flatmates had once called her the 'Ice Maiden' and were of the opinion that she had no heart, since it was they who would eventually have to hand out various excuses to the extra-persistent male. In spite of all this, their friendship was strong, and Sarah wondered if she still had a room in the flat. It was true that she often went off for long periods chasing a story, but never this long, and if someone had got her room there was the question of her things.

She sighed. They would have seen the paper, of course, and that would have explained where she had been for the past five weeks; even so, it meant some explaining on her part, and she didn't feel up to it right now.

Kathy glanced across at her. 'We'll stop at Adelaide River for a break,' she said. 'We ought to be able to get some lunch at the motel there.'

Sarah nodded abstractedly, but her mind was still on her worries.

Adelaide River was a small community in pleasant country surroundings, and as Kathy had surmised, they were able to get lunch at the small motel.

While they waited for their salad to be served in the bright dining area, Kathy, taking due note of Sarah's preoccupation, asked quietly, 'Problems?'

Sarah's eyes left the red and white checked cloth on the table and met Kathy's sympathetic brown ones, and Sarah thought how different she was from her brother, although there was some facial likeness between them. She took a deep breath. 'Five weeks is a long time,' she said. 'I did have lodgings with some friends of mine. It just means a lot of explaining——' she ended lamely.

Kathy blinked. 'As long as that?' she exclaimed. 'Good gracious! No wonder you're worried. Er—anyone special?' she asked.

Sarah got the meaning, and shook her head. 'Not in that sense,' she replied, then took another deep breath. 'Take no notice of me,' she added firmly. 'I'm just a bit disorientated, that's all. I'll be all right once I'm back.'

'And no wonder!' Kathy said indignantly. 'I know my brother, and he's not the most admirable of hosts, and he's got this thing about the press. It must have been rotten for you.'

This produced a wry smile from Sarah. 'I wasn't exactly given the red carpet treatment,' she commented dryly.

After a leisurely lunch, they were on their way again, and within an hour and a half were entering Darwin and heading for the airport.

By late evening Sarah found herself installed at Kathy's home in Rose Bay on the outskirts of Sydney. She had been no match for Kathy's determined bid to take her home, in order, as she had put it, 'to get herself acclimatised', and as she had sensibly pointed out, it was too late an hour to go wandering the city streets, not certain if she had a bed waiting for her or not.

All that could be seen to in the morning, Kathy had stated firmly, and in the meantime, she would be glad of Sarah's company as Luke was not due to return from Newcastle until late the following day.

By the time Sarah had finished breakfast the next day, she had to admit that Kathy's sensible persuasion to take her time before announcing her arrival back in Sydney had been a good one. She now felt refreshed, and more able to cope with all the small problems that she had landed herself with the day before.

All that, she told herself cheerfully, could be

easily overcome. Whether she liked it or not, she was in the news again in a big way, and all she had to do was to present herself back at the news desk and go on from there. She would, she mused, as she drank her coffee, stand by her earlier plans where her fictional engagement to Sean Cartier was concerned. She would simply tell Eddie that it had all been a mistake, and could she now get back to work.

Firstly, she would have to pay a visit to the flat. Viola worked in an office just down the street from the flat, and she would have to pop in there to announce her arrival and see if she still had her room, and if not, where her things were.

When Sarah announced her plans to Kathy, she offered to take her into the city, and Sarah gratefully accepted, considering that Kathy was going there anyway some time that day to collect provisions.

It was strange being back in her old haunts, and strange was the word, for Sarah experienced none of the expected lifts of joy as the car swept down old familiar streets, eventually stopping as near as possible to the General Post Office in Martin Place, that Sarah had asked to be dropped at, as it was only a short walk from there to Viola's office and the flat.

After promising to ring Kathy that evening and let her know how she had got on, Sarah was on her own for the first time in all those weeks, and that did give her a lift. Her head came up and chin went out, as she made her way to Viola's office.

She might only have been gone a couple of

days by the casual, 'Hi!' and grin from Viola, when Sarah walked into Reception. 'So you're back at last, and quite famous, too,' she went on chattily.

This, thought Sarah, was only the start of it, and it caused her some annoyance. She hadn't earned these tributes, and couldn't deny them either, without going into things that she wanted to forget. 'Is my room still available?' she asked. 'I'm afraid I wasn't able to contact you——'

Viola blinked at her. 'Of course it's still your room. You're getting forgetful in your old age,' she commented teasingly. 'You sent the rent, remember? Enough to cover two months. With all that excitement I suppose it went out of your mind,' she added kindly. 'Who's the boy-friend?' she asked.

It was Sarah's turn to blink. 'Boy-friend?' she repeated bewilderedly.

'Oh, come off it!' Viola said indignantly. 'That gorgeous specimen who called on us last night and told us you'd be back today.'

'If he's who I think he is, then he's certainly not my boy-friend,' Sarah replied crossly. There was only one person that could have been, and it somewhat dismayed her to learn that he was in Sydney. She had thought Canberra was the place he would have been summoned to.

Viola gave her a pitying look. 'I think you'll find that he's got other ideas. Margaret and I felt that he was giving us the once over. You know the sort of thing—were we fit company for his woman. Not that we minded, mind you, and we only wished he'd stayed longer.'

Sarah was only too happy to escape from Viola's garrulous wanderings and get to the flat. One part of her leaped for joy, and the other, the sensible side of her, reasoned that it was just the sort of thing Sean would have done. It had been entirely his fault that she had been denied her freedom, and he had probably got an eye on the future, because she could still make things difficult for him should anything come out.

As she let herself into her room and surveyed her familiar belongings, she felt an unaccountable desire to weep her heart out. She hated Sean for what he had done to her. She had been so comfortable before. All she had ever wanted was her work, nothing else had mattered to her.

She gave a ragged sob. He had only to lift his little finger and she would have rushed into his arms. She didn't care about her job any more, the only thing that mattered was that she should be with him until the end of time.

Why couldn't he have left her alone? Hadn't he done enough damage? She caught her breath. Apparently not, if he had taken the trouble to visit the flat. And it hadn't been her who had sent that rent money, either. He must have got her address from Eddie on some excuse or other.

This thought reminded her that she had still to make her visit to the paper, and it depressed her even more, but it had to be done.

She made a determined effort to pull herself together, and changing into a light cotton dress and dashing cold water over her eyelids, she combed her hair, then surveyed the result in her mirror.

As far as she could see, she was the same

person who had left her room all that time ago on an assignment. Outwardly, there was no difference; inwardly—she grabbed her shoulder bag and was out of the flat and on her way to the *Daily's* offices before she allowed herself to wallow further into the depths of misery.

It was the same as she had remembered, which was somehow surprising to her altered state of mind. Typewriters clacked in the news room, telephones rang, and the frenzied activity that was always present hit Sarah with a discordancy that shook her. Once she had belonged to this world; now she felt an alien.

Someone spotted her on the way to Eddie's office, and shouted a welcome, but Sarah after giving a wave of the hand in acknowledgement, resolutely marched on to the editor's office.

Eddie was on the phone when she walked in, but after giving her a surprised but welcoming grin, he waved an airy hand towards a chair, ended his conversation, then sat back surveying her. 'Who's a clever girl, then?' he said teasingly. 'Not only comes up with the scoop of the year, but lands the famous boffin at her feet.'

Sarah felt like hitting him with his Out Tray, but managed to quell this unkind thought. They had all been taken for a ride by that 'famous boffin', and it was about time a few facts were aired. 'I haven't got the famous boffin at my feet,' she declared between her teeth, 'and what's more, if I had, I'd kick him!' she added ferociously.

Eddie's eyes showed his amusement, which annoyed her even more. 'I take it there's been a slight hitch?' he said mildly.

'It's more in the line of a volcanic eruption,' Sarah said darkly. 'Look, you know I didn't write that story. Why did you give me the credit?' she demanded.

Eddie's plump features sobered and he looked at her over the top of his spectacles. 'You were on the spot, weren't you?' he said comfortably. 'Besides, if the big man boss hadn't taken such a shine to you, we wouldn't have been the first with the news, would we?' he pointed out reasonably, then added hastily, 'By the way, your man's at the Civic Hall today, and it's the last chance he's giving the press to interview him. After that, I gather he intends to retire back into obscurity.'

Sarah's eyes went to the In Tray. It was heavier than the Out Tray. 'He's not my man!' she ground out furiously. 'And as for retiring back into obscurity, the sooner that happens the better, as far as I'm concerned,' she declared fervently. Eddie sorted vaguely through the papers in front of him. 'Then you don't want to cover it, I gather?' he said mildly.

So he'd got there at last! Sarah thought, as she replied, 'No. Have you anything else for me?' she added hopefully.

Eddie studied her thoughtfully over the top of his glasses. 'Well, everything else is covered,' he said carefully. 'Now look here, Sarah, you go back to the flat until things are sorted out. I wasn't counting on your coming back, you see. Cartier sounded pretty definite as far as your future was concerned, and—well, he's not the type to play around, is he?'

Sarah's eyes widened as she caught the drift of his thoughts. 'Are you telling me I haven't got a job here now?' she demanded.

'Now look here,' Eddie said quietly. 'See it from my point of view. I don't want to lose you, or rather I didn't want to lose you, but I know it's just one of those things. One minute you're on the staff, the next, you're whisked off the job by a determined male who doesn't believe in working wives.' He shrugged his plump shoulders. 'If what you say is right and you have finished with Cartier, then come back and see me in a fortnight's time, and we'll discuss terms.' He fished in a drawer and drew out an envelope. 'There's two months' pay there, plus a small token of gratitude from the big chief.' He gave her a grin. 'Either way, you're covered,' he said. 'All I want is the proof that Cartier is out of the picture where your future's concerned,' he added kindly. 'Miss Dalway's retiring at the end of the month, and I'll be looking for another features editor on the women's page,' he tacked on meaningly.

Sarah wanted to throw the envelope back at him, but had to concede miserably that he had been more than fair with her. The fact that he didn't know the real reason why Sean Cartier had formed a sudden attachment to her, made things all the harder to bear, and for a moment she was tempted to reveal all, but at that precise moment the phone rang on Eddie's desk, and he was soon immersed in the daily routine once more, dismissing her with a wave of the hand.

As Sarah made her way back to the flat, she

recalled her earlier thoughts on how things would
go when she presented herself back at the
newsroom. Not once had she imagined herself
being unable to convince Eddie that the fictitious
engagement was over. People got engaged every
day of the week, didn't they, and got unengaged
just as fast. What was so very different with her?
Why shouldn't Eddie have accepted her story?

There was, she told herself bitterly, as she let
herself into her room in the flat, a very simple
answer. Sean Cartier! Not the type to play
around, was what Eddie had said.

She threw her shoulder bag on the bed. The
wretched man had them all mesmerised. She sat
down wearily on the bed. Well, he'd wanted to
put a stop to her career, and he had very nearly
succeeded, only not quite, she thought, as she
recalled Eddie's hint of a job in features.

Sarah took a deep breath. It was the only high
spot in what would otherwise be a dismal future.
She shook her head. What on earth was wrong with
her? Features editor was a plum job, and Eddie
must have thought she was capable of managing it
if he had bothered to mention it to her. He was not
given to vague meanderings on any subject. So in
point of fact, she told herself, cheering up somewhat
at the thought, the job was as good as hers.

In a very short time Eddie would have all the
proof he required concerning her future where
Sean Cartier was concerned. Within a day or so
he would be heading back to the homestead, for
Sarah was certain that that was where he would
be going. As Kathy had said, the place was ideal
as a haven from publicity.

Thinking of Kathy reminded Sarah of her promise to ring her, and as it was now almost lunchtime, she thought it was likely that she was now back at her home, and fishing out her address book for the number, she gave her a call.

After being assured by Sarah that all was well, Kathy said, 'Sean's coming to dinner this evening, Luke should be back by then. It ought to be a nice family evening, we don't see that much of Sean these days, and I was a bit put out when he said he was bringing someone with him. I've no idea who. I just hope it isn't one of those professor friends of his, or the whole evening will be spent in talk way above my head—Luke's too, come to that. On the other hand, it could be Pauline, although I sincerely hope not. She rang me a little while ago, so I know she's in Sydney— for obvious reasons, I'm afraid.'

Sarah listened politely, and after promising to ring Kathy now and again to keep in touch, rang off.

She wished Pauline all the luck in the world in landing her man. She certainly deserved some success for perseverence, she thought dryly, and wouldn't it be wonderful if their engagement could be announced before they left Sydney, because she couldn't have any better proof than that to show Eddie!

CHAPTER TEN

SARAH went to the small Italian restaurant that she and the other girls had patronised since moving into the flat, as it was only a street away.

Mario, the short stocky proprietor of the restaurant, welcomed her as a long-lost friend, and deferentially showed her to a table near the window.

The warm spring sunshine shone through the lace-draped windows and shot blades of light in between the tables, and the crisp blue and white checked tablecloths seemed to sparkle in competition with the silverware.

Sarah had no sooner started on her lasagne, a speciality of the house, and which Mario had brought her without an order, when Viola and Margaret joined her.

'Thought you'd be down at the Civic Hall,' Margaret, a tall, slim brunette, who had always to watch her figure, said, as she stared hungrily at Sarah's plate, adding, 'I wonder if I dare,' as Mario walked towards them.

Sarah was now well aware that Margaret and Viola knew the identity of the man who had called at the flat the previous evening, and she replied, 'I'm having a fortnight off.' Later, she told herself, she would put them in the picture, but she had no wish to go over it now.

'But surely——' began Viola, after casting a

doubtful glance at Margaret, 'if he's there, oughtn't you to be there, too?'

Sarah gave her an exasperated look. 'Look, apart from my having to put up with his company for the past few weeks while I was on the job, there's absolutely no reason why we should ever see each other again. It was very good of him to make sure that I had somewhere to go when I came back home, but that doesn't mean that he's my keeper,' she ended flatly.

Margaret shook her head. 'I don't get this,' she said. 'Do you?' she appealed to Viola. 'Somewhere we've missed out. By the way he acted last night, we started thinking of advertising for someone to take your room, didn't we, Vi?'

Viola nodded as she attacked her food, and there was silence for a minute or so while their appetites were assuaged. Then Margaret returned to the attack. 'Do you mean to tell us there's absolutely nothing between you and that gorgeous specimen?' she demanded.

Sarah wondered if she was ever going to be allowed to forget Sean Cartier. 'Definitely not!' she stated firmly, as she applied herself to her food again, then before any other questions were asked, she went on with, 'I'm sorry to disappoint you both, but you'll have to put up with me for some time to come, and if you don't mind, let's change the subject, because——'

Viola, who had just glanced round the room at this point, said in an awed whisper, 'I'm afraid the subject has just walked in, and unless I'm very much mistaken is heading this way.'

Sarah followed her gaze and to her intense

annoyance saw Sean walking towards them. She felt a ridiculous urge to take off, but she couldn't because it would mean asking Viola to get up too, as she couldn't get past her.

'Eddie said I'd probably find you here,' said Sean, his blue eyes on Sarah, giving her the impression that she was the only one in the room, let alone at the table!

'You've met Viola and Margaret, haven't you?' she said stiffly, inwardly furious with Eddie for his helpful suggestion as to where Sean might find her.

Sean nodded casually at the girls, and without asking permission drew another chair up to the table and joined them, making Sarah's eyes flash. 'I expected to see you at the Civic Hall,' he said, ignoring the warning signals.

'Oh, she's on a fortnight's holiday,' Margaret supplied helpfully, now finding Sarah's fire directed at her.

'I expect I shall read all about it tomorrow,' Sarah managed to murmur casually. 'Are you off now?' she asked hopefully. 'Eddie told me you're not going to be available after today.'

'That depends,' Sean said casually, and Sarah felt rather than saw Margaret's swift glance at Viola, that made her dig a little too ferociously into her fruit salad.

Mario then appeared on the scene, and Sean settled for the same as the girls, leaving Sarah to bide her time, because the girls would soon have to depart back to work, and she filled in the time by surreptitiously studying the man who had blighted her life.

He was certainly an impressive-looking man, and Sarah, who had never seen him in a city suit before, could well understand the girls' only too apparent appreciation of his company. They didn't know the half of it, she thought darkly, and she wondered how long they would put up with his high-handed ways, or with the veiled insults she had had to suffer at his hands.

At last Margaret and Viola could linger no longer, and Sarah knew they had cut it fine to get back to work on time, and after a regretful farewell to Sean, and favouring Sarah with a look that plainly said, 'We'll see you later. Just who do you think you're kidding?' they were on their way.

For a few seconds, silence fell between Sarah and Sean. Sarah did not think it was fair for a man to be attacked while he was enjoying his meal so she waited until he had refused a sweet and ordered coffee, before wading in with, 'I've had enough trouble convincing Eddie that I'm ready to start work, without your putting ideas into my friends' heads as well!'

'What sort of ideas?' Sean enquired lazily, his eyes lightly scanning her indignant features.

'You know very well!' Sarah spat out at him. 'He actually believed all that stuff and nonsense you gave him about our being engaged, and no thanks to you, I almost lost my job!'

'Almost?' purred Sean.

'Almost,' confirmed Sarah. 'Instead, it's very likely I shall take over as features editor at the end of the month, so really,' she gave him an acid smile, 'I suppose you did me a favour. They say every cloud has a silver lining, don't they?' she added sweetly.

'If we weren't in such a public place, I might just attempt to alter your thinking on that,' he said casually, but his eyes belied his nonchalance. 'It's a pity about that job, but you're not taking it.'

Sarah's hand closed round the strap of her shoulder bag so hard that she could feel the leather thong of the strap biting into her palm as she rose from the table. 'If you don't mind,' she said icily, 'I've finished my lunch, and I really have to go now.'

To her further fury, she found her wrist caught by Sean's strong fingers. 'You'll go, we'll both go, when I'm ready. Have another cup of coffee,' he suggested lightly, 'and stop acting like a frightened filly.'

Sarah was forced to sit down again, but drew the line at more coffee. 'Why can't you leave me alone?' she said in a low voice.

Sean's blue eyes met hers. 'Don't you know?' he asked mockingly.

Sarah looked away as she felt a flush staining her cheeks. How did she cope with this man? she asked herself hopelessly. He was too experienced for her, and she had always thought herself quite knowledgeable where men were concerned. To his way of thinking she had got off lightly, and he wasn't about to give in so easily. That he wanted an affair with her was clear. Would he suggest that they go back to the homestead? Thanks to Margaret, he knew she had a fortnight's holiday.

'You want to take me back to the homestead?'

she asked bluntly. 'Is that what you meant when you said "it depends" when I asked you when you were going back?'

Sean's eyes searched hers. 'Would you come?' he challenged.

It was the answer that Sarah had expected, but even so, she felt a dull ache inside her. 'You'd do much better with Pauline,' she said quietly.

'It's not Pauline I want. It's you,' he replied, his eyes never leaving her face.

She stared down at the tablecloth. Well, at least it was out now. She had known it all along.

'We're having dinner with Kathy,' he said, as if everything was settled. 'I've got lumbered with an appointment at three, but I should be through by four,' he told her, as he placed some notes on the table to pay for the meal, and waited for her to join him. 'I'll pick you up at six. I suppose you'll need some time to pack,' he added lightly. 'We can take one of the night flights out.'

Sarah felt like a leaf that had fallen into a fast-flowing river and was being borne along willy-nilly to some unknown destination as Sean escorted her to the flat, keeping up a light conversation about how he was looking forward to the peace and quiet of the homestead and couldn't shake the dust of the city off his feet fast enough, eventually leaving the utterly bemused Sarah staring after his tall figure when he left her at the door of the flat.

As soon as he had gone the spell left her, and she let herself into the flat shaking her head to clear the last remnants of fog from her senses. Either he was mad, or she was. He really thought that all he had to do was to snap his fingers and she would be there!

It did not suit her at that particular moment to call to mind that there had been a time, only that morning, in fact, when she would have been only too happy to have had the chance.

It was small wonder that Sean had no trouble with women! With his caveman style of courting, they didn't stand a chance! He mesmerised them first, just as he had mesmerised Viola and Margaret—but not this female, she told herself stoutly, as she went into her room.

'I'm a successful journalist,' she announced to the room, 'and I've got the chance of a lifetime to move on in my profession, and I'm taking it, do you hear?' she demanded of the baby koala bear sitting on her dressing table, and whose large soft glass eyes seemed to wink back at her. 'We know what's what, don't we?' she went on firmly. 'Just for once he's picked on the wrong number. No man tells us what to do, do they? Am I to throw everything away on a light affair with a man who happens to fancy me? Well, I'm not!'

At this point Sarah suddenly recalled that she was talking to herself, and shut her eyes. It was a good thing that the girls weren't in, or they'd be making an appointment at the funny farm for her, she thought grimly.

She sat down on her bed. She wasn't sure they wouldn't do so anyway, after she asked them to tell Sean Cartier that she was out when he called for her at six.

Not once during all that time had she given him any encouragement to think she would be willing to have an affair with him. The opposite, in fact, she thought, going over their association at the base, and then on to the stay at the homestead.

A few seconds later she gave a light groan, as she recalled the bedroom scene when she had invited Sean to help her into the nightdress he had brought her.

He had said something about 'taking her up on that later,' hadn't he? and now he hoped to collect!

Well, hope was as far as it was going, she thought, as she glanced at her wrist watch. It was just past two-thirty, and she had three clear hours before the girls came back from work, and several things to do.

A short time later Sarah had packed all she needed for a week's stay. She knew precisely where she was going. Mrs Smith, the office cleaner, had obliged her once before when she was on the run from a particularly persistent male who had haunted her existence, until he finally got the message that there was nothing doing.

The next thing on the agenda was to write two letters, one to the girls, and the other to Sean Cartier.

She told the girls that she had decided to spend a week at a holiday resort, possibly a fortnight, but she'd see how it went. She also mentioned that Sean would be calling at six, and would they please give him the note she had left for him.

That done, she settled down to her last task, the letter to Sean, in which she explained that since she had left him, she had had second thoughts about spending a few weeks with him, and hoped he would not be too disappointed, and after thanking him politely for the offer, she wished him a good journey home.

After she had propped the two letters on the hall table where the girls couldn't fail to see them, she picked up her case and left the flat before she changed her mind.

She was lucky in getting a taxi to take her to the inner suburban area where Mrs Smith lived, and within fifteen minutes was drawing up outside the high-rise block of flats and making her way to number twenty-five on the ground floor.

'That pesky man turned up again?' Mrs Smith asked cheerfully, as she welcomed Sarah into her small living room. 'Time you got married, duck, that'll put an end to these sort of capers,' she added in her unmistakably Cockney accent, because Mrs Smith had been born in London, and although she had spent the last ten years in Sydney, the other side of the world, she had never dropped the accent, and woe betide anyone who attempted to make her.

Sarah did not feel too inclined to go into deeper detail, but let Mrs Smith presume that it was the same 'pesky man' rather than tell her that it was another one!

Although Mrs Smith had gone to Australia after she had become a widow, to be with her son who had settled out there with his family, from what Sarah had gathered, it had not been an ideal move, and as time had gone on family visits had got fewer, but being the cheerful and outgoing soul that she was, she made light of what must at times have been a lonely existence for her. She was not short of friends, and looked after a couple of old ladies along the passage from her flat, doing odd jobs and bringing shopping back for them on her way home from her chores at the *Daily* offices.

Having already spent a few days with her, Sarah now knew the routine, and made sure that she did not put her out of her usual routine, although last time it had been different, as Sarah had still been working then, and had left for work before Mrs Smith returned home.

Sarah had been quite firm in her resolve not to make work for Mrs Smith, and allowed her to give her breakfast and dinner only, since she would be cooking for herself in the evening anyway. But midday lunch, Sarah had told her firmly, would be taken in the small café across the way. She had had to tread warily, though, for Mrs Smith had her pride, and since Sarah was paying for her keep it was as well not to make too big a thing of it.

In the end Sarah won her case, for she happened to know that Mrs Smith provided snacks for her two old friends down the corridor, as she had once confided to Sarah. 'They don't bother, you know, and as long as I know they've had something, I don't worry. That social lot are always snooping around to find out how they're coping. They're not ready for the ladies' rest home yet, as nice as they're made out to be. Still,' she admitted grudgingly, 'I suppose they're only doing their bit. Got nothing else to do, most of them, they're a bit on the lah-di-dah side for me, though,' she declared.

So Sarah settled in, and the evening was spent in gossiping, although around six o'clock she found herself glancing at the much battered old mantelpiece clock that Mrs Smith had brought from her old home in London, stating that it brought back happy memories for her, and they could keep those fancy timepieces that no one could mend when they went wrong. That clock had gone on for nigh on forty years, and would see her out.

But none of these sentiments were on Sarah's mind when the hands pointed to six. In her mind's eyes she was back at the flat, trying to gauge Sean's reaction to her letter, and she felt grateful that she was nowhere in the vicinity to receive the backlash her words would invoke.

She was also glad that she had had the foresight to tell the girls that she was at a holiday resort, because that could be anywhere, and would completely mislead them as to her real abode.

Would he still keep the dinner date with Kathy? she wondered. She thought he would, as she felt he would keep to his original plan of taking a night flight out to Darwin.

The trouble was, there was nothing certain where that man was concerned, and Sarah preferred to be safe rather than sorry—and she would be sorry, she was certain of that. She would never forgive herself for losing the opportunity of a lifetime to indulge in an affair that would leave her with lasting scars.

As she sat in Mrs Smith's small sitting room, listening to the clatter going on in her small kitchen while her hostess set about getting their evening meal, singing lustily at the top of her voice, for Mrs Smith was much addicted to singing, and as she had once said, 'It keeps me cheerful, dearie,' it did nothing to lighten Sarah's depression, only somehow deepened it. It would be a long time before she felt like singing about anything.

Being an early riser because of her job, Mrs Smith was always tucked up in bed by ten at the latest, and Sarah followed her example, although Mrs Smith had expected her to stay and see the rest of the television programme through, but Sarah had had enough for one day—and what a day! she thought tiredly as she took a quick shower before going to bed in the small second bedroom of the flat.

As nice as the room was, it was completely impersonal, and she thought longingly of her own room, that she should have been sleeping in for the first time since her fateful departure for Darwin and the camp.

That wretched man had a lot to answer for, she told herself indignantly as she settled herself in bed. Kathy had never made a truer statement than when she had sympathised with her about not having much luck with her family.

She hadn't known the half of it, Sarah mused, as she lay waiting for sleep. Right now, she was probably wondering why Sean was in such a foul mood, and why he hadn't brought his guest to dinner, and Sarah couldn't see him coming clean on that one. It was not the sort of thing you told a sister, and as he would reasonably not be

expecting to see her for a few more months,
something that would never come to light. No,
she thought drowsily, he would say something
about someone letting him down at the last
moment, and leave it at that.

Having told Mrs Smith that she was on a few
days' holiday, Sarah was free to follow her own
inclinations during the day, and shortly after ten
the next morning she left the flat, intending to take
a bus down to the harbour, a busy bustling area
where it was unlikely that she would meet anyone
that she knew, but which would provide her with
some entertainment to while away the time.

Halfway along the corridor, she was startled to
hear her name called, and even more alarmed to
see Kathy standing next to one of the doors and
about to ring the bell. 'So it is you!' said Kathy,
as she walked towards her. 'Oh, dear, don't say
one of my old ladies has been robbed, or even
murdered! I can't think of any other reason for
your being here,' she added worriedly.

Having assured her on this point, Sarah went
on to explain that she was just visiting one of the
Daily's staff, and left it at that.

'Well, that's a relief,' said Kathy. 'Perhaps I'd
better leave the visit. It's not my day for calling,
but as I was in the neighbourhood I thought I'd
save myself a journey tomorrow. It wasn't a good
idea, anyway, they don't exactly look forward to
our visits, you know. They're convinced we're
about to drag them off to the rest home, which is
all nonsense, of course. As long as they're coping
we're only too happy to keep them in their own
homes.'

To Sarah's discomfort, she accompanied her on her way out. She liked Kathy, but this was one time she wished her elsewhere, and she couldn't help miserably wondering why fate seemed to have it in for her.

'Look, I'm dying for a coffee,' said Kathy. 'Have you got time to have one with me? There's a small café across the road here that I usually patronise when I'm in this area. I don't like to put the old people to the trouble of making me anything.'

If there was anything that Sarah did not want it was to stay in Kathy's company, but considering that it was she who had come to her rescue the day before, and Sarah was of the opinion that if she hadn't she would still be stuck back at the homestead, she consented to join her, and as they walked towards the café it did occur to Sarah that she might hear whether Sean had left for Darwin, in which case she could come out of hiding.

'I was a little surprised to see you,' Kathy told her, as they settled at a table. 'I had an idea you'd be taking a few days off,' and at Sarah's sharp glance at her, she added, 'I don't know where I got that idea—probably thought you'd earned it, I suppose,' she added with a grin. 'What's it like being back in harness again?' she asked lightly.

For a split second it went through Sarah's mind to lie, but something told her that it would mean more lies following about what case she had been working on, etc, and she was too tired of subterfuge to want to go through all that, so she settled for the truth. 'Well, as a matter of fact, you were right. I am taking a few days off,' she admitted reluctantly.

'Oh, splendid!' Kathy said, 'and I've got nothing on for the rest of the day. First, you must come back with me, I've got a lovely tongue salad already prepared in the fridge, so it's no trouble, and we can laze in the garden after lunch. That's if you've nothing else on?' she enquired anxiously. 'I was dreading going back home with Luke out all day. It always catches me after I've spent a week or so in company, until I get back into routine.'

There was definitely a touch of Sean in the way his sister was arranging things, Sarah thought dispiritedly, and her heart ached for him. Perhaps it was the fact that he had actually been at Kathy's house the previous evening that settled it for her, and she allowed herself to be talked into going back with Kathy. What did it matter anyway, she asked herself, certain now that he had gone back. After this, she would not see Kathy again. It would be part of her life that would remain a closed chapter. It had to be, if she was to go on living with any expectation of happiness.

As soon as they arrived at Kathy's house, Sarah was told to make herself comfortable in the large luxurious lounge while Kathy made a phone call. 'I'm not sure what time Luke's coming back,' she explained. 'Sometimes he has to take a client out to dinner, and it's easier for me to phone him, he's so busy.'

Sarah picked up a magazine while she waited for Kathy to return, but soon her eyes wandered round the well furnished lounge. They would have had coffee in here after dinner, she thought, and she wondered which chair Sean had taken.

Her breath caught in a ragged sob, and for one blind unreasoning moment she considered telling Kathy everything, but her pride held her back. Kathy would give her the same good advice that she had given herself—to keep her distance, and that she had done the right thing in turning Sean's offer down.

Kathy had seemed a long time on the phone, but when she returned, she told Sarah she had slipped through to the kitchen and got their lunch ready after she had made the call, and all they had to do was enjoy it.

It certainly looked appetising, with crisp lettuce hearts and the accompanying ingredients, but such was Sarah's misery that she found it hard to do it justice. It had been a mistake to come here, she told herself, as she made an effort to reply to Kathy's bright observations in the same vein.

Having decided that she shouldn't have come, all Sarah wanted was an excuse to leave as soon after lunch as possible without upsetting Kathy, and as they reached the coffee stage, back in the lounge, the sound of a vehicle pulling up outside the house gave Sarah a feeling that perhaps help was at hand. It was obviously a friend of Kathy's who had decided to pay her a visit, and would give her an excuse to leave. She could always remember something she had meant to do. It wasn't as if she had arranged to meet Kathy.

When Kathy slipped out to meet the caller,

Sarah began to think up various plausible reasons as to why she should take her leave. It would just be a matter of calling for a taxi, and keeping up polite conversation with Kathy and her friend until it arrived.

In the event, no such plausible excuses were required, at least not on that subject, for when the door was suddenly flung open she found herself facing an irate Sean, who closed the door behind him with a firm snap that lent ominous undertones to the action.

'Just what the devil are you playing at?' he demanded angrily. 'I realise it's a woman's prerogative to change her mind, but you might have had the decency to tell me that you didn't intend going through with it, instead of taking the coward's way out!'

Sarah, slowly recovering from the shock of seeing him, took a deep breath. Of all the nerve—what chance had she had of putting her point of view forward? 'Because you didn't give me the chance,' she retorted, now as angry as he was.

Sean's eyes narrowed, and he folded his arms across his chest. 'Okay, so now I'm giving you the chance—and don't give me that stuff about being a career woman, because it just won't wear,' he warned her.

There was nothing like having the floor taken from under you, Sarah thought bitterly, for that had been her mainstay, that she was a career woman and intended to remain one. 'Look,' she said wearily, 'right from the start you accused me of first ruining Don's life, and if that wasn't enough, of deliberately setting out to ruin others.

I'm pretty certain where you got those impressions from, but never once did you give me the benefit of the doubt. And now——' she swallowed, pushing down the temptation to scream at him, 'you have the nerve to wonder why I'm refusing to have an affair with you, and if you think I'm throwing away everything I've worked for, for all these years, then, as I've told you before, you've got the wrong number!'

Sean's blue eyes widened as the impact of her words hit him. 'Just where did you get the idea that I played fast and loose in the petticoat line?' he demanded harshly.

Sarah looked into his blazing eyes. 'From a colleague of mine,' she retorted coldly.

'It wasn't Charles Ashley, by any chance, was it?' Sean asked silkily. 'He's already got the beaut of a black eye for past services, and if it was, I'll take great pleasure in closing the other eye!'

Sarah felt a twinge of sympathy for Charles at this point. 'As a matter of fact, it was a woman,' she told him, and that was as much as she was prepared to say.

'And you believed her?' Sean demanded.

'As you believed Charles,' she reminded him angrily.

Sean's blue eyes had an amused glint in them as he looked at her. 'Touché,' he said softly. 'For your information, I've got a padre calling at the homestead a week from today. I can see now that I wasn't exactly explicit as to my intentions. I got the impression that you were as aware as I was that there could only be one ending where we were concerned. Even if it meant kidnapping you all over again, but I couldn't make a move until that report came out, you were so mad at me you might have let the cat out of the bag without realising it.'

'You quite deliberately gave me that information, didn't you?' Sarah accused him roundly, not ready yet to forgive him.

Sean grinned wickedly at her. 'Can you tell me how I could have kept you near me, if I hadn't?' he queried softly. 'I told you that Don had fallen for you like a ton of bricks, didn't I? Well, the truth was that it was myself that I was talking about. I knew you were my woman as soon as I set eyes on you.' His fine mouth twisted wryly. 'I should have known that Ashley was after you himself. As it was, all I could think of was that Don had fallen into the same trap, and the idea of your being engaged to another man, even though it was my cousin, was totally unthinkable, but I couldn't let you go. I guess I've got Kathy to thank for putting me into the picture where Don was concerned, so I won't,' he told her grandly, 'hold your unwarranted suspicions of my intentions where you're concerned against you. I have no wish for an affair with you, or to have a common law wife,' his eyes met hers. 'This is for keeps. I've got you now, and I'm keeping you.'

He moved forward purposefully to take her in his arms, and Sarah, with her eyes on his tall straight figure, still attired in his city suit, had time to wonder how she could have mistaken his obvious sincerity, and gave a thankful thought for Kathy, for she knew that it had been Sean that she had rung and not her husband.

With Sean's strong arms around her, she gave up all pretence of holding out on him. Within a week they were to be married, and she still couldn't believe it. 'What will happen when you go back to work?' she demanded, when he gave her a breathing space.

'You come with me,' he said huskily, nuzzling her cheek. 'What do you think I trained you for back at the camp? Besides, I don't trust you. You have a nasty habit of running out on me. I want you where I can see you all the time,' and he endorsed this sentiment with a devastating kiss.

A little while later, Sarah had recovered sufficiently enough to tease him a little. 'And I was so looking forward to being the features editor on the women's page,' she murmured naughtily.

'The only magazine you're going to feature in will be *Mother and Baby*,' Sean assured her in no uncertain manner!

In the midst of the pink haze around her, Sarah suddenly thought of Lin, and his confident prophecy that she would be back. 'Well, at least Lin will be pleased to hear that I'm an honest woman,' she sighed dreamily.

Sean's expressive brows raised in query at this.

'He thought I'd stolen something from you,' she explained.

He held her closer. 'Well, you did, didn't you?' he said softly, then with his lips on hers, whispered, 'Thief!'

Coming Next Month in Harlequin Romances!

2749   A MATTER OF MARNIE   Rosemary Badger
Convincing an Australian construction tycoon that his
grandmother has been neglected is a formidable task. Living with
him in order to care for the woman is an even greater challenge.

2750   THE PERFECT CHOICE   Melissa Forsythe
A voice student in Vienna seldom turns men's heads. So when a
handsome stranger woos her, she's in too deep by the time she
discovers his motive for choosing her over her beautiful friend.

2751   SAFE HARBOUR   Rosalie Henaghan
This trustworthy secretary weathers her boss's changeable moods
until his woman friend predicts an end to Anna's working days—
and sets out to make her prophecy come true.

2752   NEVER THE TIME AND THE PLACE   Betty Neels
The consulting surgeon at a London hospital disturbs his ward sister's
natural serenity. She's having enough trouble coping with a broken
engagement without having to put up with his arrogance.

2753   A WILL TO LOVE   Edwina Shore
That the family's Queensland homestead should be sold is
unthinkable. But the only way to save it—according to her
grandfather's will—is to marry the same man who rejected her
four years ago.

2754   HE WAS THE STRANGER   Sheila Strutt
The manager of Milk River Ranch knew that a male relative would
inherit her uncle's spread. But why did the beneficiary have to be a
writer who would either sell out or take over completely?

Can you keep a secret?

You can keep this one plus 4 free novels